THE BOOK GLASSES

ARTHUR BOZIKAS

ACKNOWLEDGMENTS

I would like to thank those who helped to make this book possible. Special thanks to my wife, Helen, and our children, Jimmy and Pamela, for their dedicated love and support, and to both our parents and all our immediate family for their tireless affections.

Arthur

ALSO BY ARTHUR BOZIKAS

BLACK OPS: ZULU. Tom Stiles Thrillers, Book 1

LEGEND OF THE HOLY FATHER'S
BOOK GLASSES

According to myth, a pair of eyeglasses were crafted in Rome
over two and a half centuries ago for the pope from a stone sent
by God. It was understood that whoever had the good fortune
to wear these glasses was blessed with superior vision.
However, their real power was revealed when the wearer of the
glasses was reading a book. The reader was given unmeasurable
wisdom and knowledge beyond belief.

The *Occhiali da vista* scrolls of Pope Leo XIII from the
1881 Vatican Secret Archives, now missing, were rumoured to
have told the story of this pair of book glasses commissioned
between 1700 and 1800 by the Papal Basilica of St Peter for
the sole use of the pope and all future popes. The lenses were
to be crafted from a unique clear stone, rumoured to be blessed
by angels. The origin of the stone was unknown but renowned
experts at the time all agreed that it hadn't come from the
ground. Instead, one autumn day after morning prayers, the
stone had suddenly appeared in the Vatican City centre—a gift
from the heavens above after a hailstorm. Apart from the
unnamed cardinal who found it, only a few individuals, high in

the inner circle of the Catholic church, knew of the stone and its origin. No other reference to this event was ever recorded, before or after this time.

Experts who examined the stone were sworn to secrecy. Not even the sitting pope, Pope Benedict XIV, knew about it. Secrecy was paramount and death would befall anyone who dared even talk about it. This curse of death was common knowledge and thus, silence was respected and the existence of the extraordinary stone, and subsequently the glasses into which it was crafted, remained hidden from the world.

All documents that referred to the Holy Father's book glasses disappeared from the records. Only the myth endured, but, fearing the curse, people still do not dare speak openly about the book glasses.

PROLOGUE

Friday, 22nd August 1919

A bitterly cold gale came out of nowhere, whistling down the streets and stirring up the fallen snow, forcing the young corporal out of his shadowy vantage point to take shelter from the storm in the nearest establishment open on such a harsh winter's night.

Before crossing the threshold, he looked over his shoulder, but the Munich street was empty, its covering of snow taking on an eerie glow in the darkness.

Once in The Bavarian, the soldier, constantly on alert, scanned the room as he walked up to the bar and ordered a warm beer. Yet he noticed that every eye in the room furtively followed his movements. The packed local was full of people desperate not to be seen on this stormy subzero night and they were highly suspicious of strangers.

Without looking up, he paid the barman, picked up his beer and made his way back to an empty chair near the entrance.

They watch me, but not with the prestige I deserve. How

3

dare they glare at me like that? Keeping his head down, he struggled to control his mounting anger and his hand started to shake, almost spilling his beer. Could no one give him the respect he was due? He was a decorated war hero, yet these nobodies ignored him.

One day they would acknowledge him. He knew he was destined for greatness. As for his army career, what would it take to rise through the ranks? He glanced at the two-bar chevron on his uniform sleeve with distaste; it was humiliating to still be a corporal after all his faithful service. He should have been promoted well before now, but his superiors were blind idiots who could not see his true brilliance.

One day, they would do his bidding. And that day could not come soon enough.

He approached the only table with an empty chair. A man also sat there. "Excuse me, is this seat taken?" the corporal asked politely.

The well-dressed man looked up and smiled. "Please sit down. I would enjoy the company. What's your name, corporal?"

"Adolf, sir. Adolf Hitler." He sat opposite him in the window seat.

"I am Anton Drexler. Pleased to meet you. Warm in here, *ja voll?*"

"*Ja*, but it's getting bad out there."

"What's a corporal doing out this late at night?"

"My job keeps me busy working all sorts of hours, sir."

"And what is your job, may I ask?"

"Intelligence agent for the reconnaissance unit of the Reichswehr."

"Intelligence agent, you say?" He nodded. "Very impressive, young man, but what good is that now? It's 1919. The war ended last year." He slapped his beer glass against the corporal's before taking another drink and drowning his loud burst of laughter.

The soldier raised his glass to his lips, but didn't drink, and put the glass back down on the table. "Sir, I know who you are. May I suggest a few things to you? I hope you don't mind."

"So, you know I'm the chairman of the German Workers' Party, do you?"

"Yes sir, I do!" Forgetting where he was, he took his glasses out of his inside jacket pocket and put them on. When he realised what he had done, he hoped Drexler wouldn't notice them. His lapse in judgement made his heart race but he remained stone cold on the outside, concealing his discomfort at revealing his new eyeglasses with their distinctive engraved metal frames.

"What an unusual pair of eyeglasses you have. Are they army issue?"

"No, they're mine. I got them abroad, and they do the job." He hastily took them off and returned them to his jacket pocket.

"Well then, go ahead and tell me what's on your mind. I need to go soon, so hurry up."

His hand closed over the notebook in his side jacket pocket, but he let go of it, deciding to wing it without reading from his notes. Taking a deep breath, he said, "Thank you, sir. It's about communicating to the masses. I believe all effective... er... messages should be limited to a small number of points and that your party's slogan should be inserted into every speech or message until every last member of the public understands what you want him to understand by it." He picked up his drink again and waited patiently for Drexler's response.

"Very interesting, but what masses? We only have fifty-four members."

"That's what I'm talking about, sir. You don't have a clear message to draw in a crowd."

"But we are only a new party. These things take time, young man."

"Sir, fifty-four members is a good start. I would like to be your next member."

"You're a corporal in the army. How could you be a member of the German Workers' Party? Stop now and drink up. Look, you haven't touched your beer."

"I've already discharged myself from the army and I want to utilise my knowledge for a good cause. I could help you better support workers to get back their rights. All you need are more members, and I am good at communicating with people. What do you think? Are you after more members, sir?"

"You'll need to trim that moustache first. I can't have you attending looking like you're still in the trenches. It's a working man's party, understand?"

"Yes sir, the moustache will be trimmed."

"*Ja*, I tell you what, our next meeting is on September twelfth, and we get all new members to give a speech on their first night. Do you know where we meet?"

The soldier nodded.

"So, come and have your say and let's see what you can offer. I can't promise you anything. The worst thing is that you become a member of the German Workers' Party."

"Thank you, sir. And I can guarantee you will be impressed with my speech."

"If you are as confident at the meeting as you are now, we have nothing to worry about. Now drink up. Here's to you, Adolf Hitler, and to civilian life!"

Drexler knocked back the last of his beer, nodded at his companion, got up from his chair, put on his coat and hat, and walked out into the intensifying blizzard without any hesitation. Hitler remained seated in front of his untouched beer, feeling euphoric at obtaining Drexler's personal invitation to attend his next party meeting. He intended to infiltrate the party and he was off to a good start.

He pushed his full glass of beer to one side and pulled out his latest prized possession—a pair of medieval-looking reading glasses he had found a couple of years earlier while stationed on the western front. Having only recently discovered the powers of the glasses, he regularly took them out of his secret strongbox where he hid them away for safe-keeping and used them every chance he got, with extraordinary results.

After placing them back on, he took out his notebook and recorded some ideas for his first speech. He was on his way to fulfilling his plan to entrench himself in the party and provide himself with a platform from which to get his views across to the masses.

Hitler's relentless surveillance over the last few weeks had exposed Drexler's daily routines and personal habits. Arriving at the chairman's favourite drinking spot at almost the time for him to leave and go home for his usual Friday night late dinner had been masterful. He hadn't suspected a thing and was oblivious to the fact that he had followed him for almost three weeks.

The bait was set and, with the eyeglasses in his possession, Hitler was ready to execute his strategy to get an audience and thus the respect that he deserved as a first step to achieving complete control.

WINDOW DRESSING

Monday, 26th August 2013

Samantha Page turned to view her reflection one last time in the department store window as she rushed out on to the busy street with the bustling city crowd. As she admired herself in the full glare of the morning sun, flicking her hair up with one hand in a swift action from side to side, styling it the way she liked it, she tried to block out the nasty comments from people walking by who felt she was obstructing their path.

She was caught up by her imposing mirror image in almost blinding brightness, sending her mind into doubtful thoughts. She looked okay, but would it make any difference this time?

"You are fucking stupid and have no friends, you loser."

The words echoed in her head and hurt every bit as much as they had the first time she'd heard them. She'd endured a lot at the hands of her foster parents but her time with them had helped her master the art of concealing any evidence of the hard knocks that life had inflicted on her.

Sam put up a defiant front for the world. Twenty-three

9

years of failure had not destroyed her. She carefully hid the fact she had spent her entire childhood in foster care, had not graduated from high school and had never had a permanent job.

Unfortunately, her situation hadn't got any easier as the years had passed. Surviving on leftover food from the local women's refuge where she volunteered had been harrowing, and hunger left her with no choice but to endure.

Maybe this time would be different.

It was the second day of summer—a beautiful clear Sydney morning with a marble blue sky—as she walked along the busy streets in her borrowed red high heels, short white dress, red belt, and off-white handbag.

For good luck, she was wearing her best owl earrings with the tiny light blue stones for eyes that matched her own. Her long brown hair was neatly secured in a hairclip. It didn't matter that her makeup and nails had only been partially done at the sampling counter of the nearby high-end department store—nothing was going to get in the way of her 11 a.m. appointment. She would get this job and start living her dreams, believing a utopia of endless possibilities lay in wait for her.

As far back as she could remember, she had wanted to travel all over Australia, but the furthest she had ever got was Manly via Circular Quay and it had taken her almost a year to save the money for the ferry ticket. Many times, since that day, she had walked up to the Quay and fondly recalled her trip, hoping to take another ferry ride once she secured a full-time job. She had been living in the same one-bedroom unit since moving from her last foster parents' house on her eighteenth birthday. Her unemployment benefits just covered her rent and utilities, but there was nothing left for anything else.

And she couldn't get a job. Preparing for interviews had always been her downfall. It wasn't that she couldn't read, but the words were all jumbled around and hard for her to decipher. Doctors and specialists asked too many questions and didn't give any helpful answers.

She picked up the pace and was in front of the building with thirty minutes to spare. Feeling confident, she entered the utilitarian structure and gracefully stepped onto the travelator. A cheeky gust of wind came out of nowhere and prompted her to hold her skirt down.

At the top, she disembarked the travelator with a charming skip and a hop and headed to the front desk of the lobby in high spirits.

"Good morning, can I help you?" asked the concierge.

"Yes please, I'm here for my 11 a.m. interview with Brown Department Stores. I'm a little early," replied Sam.

"I'm sorry, but they're not accepting any further applications."

"No, you must be mistaken. My name is Samantha Page. I have an 11 a.m. appointment. Please check."

"You're here for the window dressing position?"

"Yes, that's it."

"Yep, people have been waiting since six this morning and they are not accepting any more applicants, sorry."

"But I have an appointment for—"

"Please contact the person you spoke to about the position. Who's next, please?"

Shoulders hunched and red-faced, Sam quickly exited the building. She felt as if everyone was looking at her and laughing. Shattered beyond belief, she hit a new low point in her life and climbing back out of it would take a miracle.

THE OLD WOMAN

Sam made it out of the building on one full breath, covering her face with one hand. She had gone about three blocks before realising she was heading toward the refuge. Paralysed with fear, she stopped, then calmed herself, and continued down the street.

Consumed with grief, she pushed past the staff, volunteers and homeless women congregating in the great hall, preparing for lunch. After almost knocking over a few women in her path, she finally found herself alone in the toilets and gave in to her despair.

"It's okay, darling. It's okay. Tell me what's upsetting you, sweetheart," said a benevolent, gentle voice from behind her.

Startled, she quickly looked up. A woman stood behind her. Sam was taken aback, almost shocked, by her appearance. She was a little shorter than Sam with startling deep brown, almost black, eyes. She looked derelict, dressed in a style long gone out of fashion. Her feet were bare. Her dress had bolero style panels at the shoulders with a sweetheart neckline and the bodice was lined to the waist, over a circle skirt.

Sam recognised the style from watching *Happy Days* reruns, but the dresses on TV never looked this dull, torn, or raggedy. "Sorry, I thought I was alone," she said.

"That's okay, love, I'm used to people not seeing me," the old woman said with a short laugh. "Now tell me what's wrong."

"I haven't seen you here before. Are you new?" asked Sam as she dried her eyes.

"No, but I've seen you, Samantha Page."

"How do you know my name?"

"Everyone here knows you, my darling. Who did your makeup?"

"Why do you ask?" Sam turned to face the mirror and they both burst into uncontrollable laughter. "They didn't show me my entire face in the mirror. They only showed me parts of it!" Sam spluttered, between laughs.

"Who did?" the old woman asked.

"The department store's makeup and beauty assistant."

"Stop it. You didn't know you were walking around the city with makeup on only half your face?"

"I went to a job interview like this!"

Despite trying hard to keep each other upright, both women slumped to the bathroom floor, laughing uproariously, bringing Sister Sue into the room to see what was going on. Sister Sue managed the day-to-day operations of the refuge for the Catholic church. Her lined face frowned at them until she realised who it was, but her blue eyes sparkled with kindness.

"Samantha, I didn't realise you were here." Her eyes twitched to her companion.

"I'm sorry, Sister Sue, were we making too much noise?"

She waved her hand dismissively. "It's all right. I just wasn't sure what was going on. I'll leave you to it."

Again, glancing at the woman with her, the sister went back to her work.

Sam and the woman picked themselves up off the floor and composed themselves, the poor old lady hacking out a nasty cough. As Sam washed off her half-done makeup, she filled her in on her disastrous morning. "I went for an interview at Brown Department Stores. They said to come at eleven, but people had apparently been turning up since six! The job was long gone by the time I got there."

The old woman patted her hand where it rested in the edge of the washbasin, recovered from her coughing fit. "Never mind. I'm sure you'll get the next job."

"That's just it," said Sam in despair. "I can't get a job. I've tried and tried."

"It will happen."

She shook her head. "But all jobs require reading and I'm not that good at it. It's no use. I'll never get a job."

The old woman waved a business card in front of her. Once Sam had dried her hands, the card was placed in her hand. "Here you go, my darling. I would like you to have this."

"What is it?"

"It's a business card of an old friend. His name is Charles Harman and he's the director and CEO of the Australian Museum. I want you to go see him about a job and tell him Joyce Thomas sent you."

"No, I couldn't possibly. Not after what just happened!"

"Don't be silly. You go, girl, and don't look back. You want a job, don't you?"

"Yes, but what will I say?"

"Just answer his questions, that's all. Off you go."

Miraculously, Sam started to feel confident that she could go to the museum and ask to see Mr Harman. Maybe she could even answer his questions. "I'll go now, Joyce. I'll do it, thank you!" She straightened herself up and turned around for one more look in the mirror.

"No, wait. Have lunch first and please fix your makeup, silly!" Joyce said with a wink.

Too excited and nervous to be hungry, Sam consumed half a salad sandwich and washed it down with a cup of weak tea and got the sisters to help fix her makeup. Then she headed for the museum, full of expectations.

———

Sister Sue watched as Sam left, hope in her heart. Joyce seemed confident that Charles would accept her recommendation and give Sam a job. Oh, if only it could be so easy! It would be the first luck Sam had ever experienced since arriving in Sydney on her eighteenth birthday.

The sound of coughing distracted her—deep wracking coughs. She sought out a dark corner of the refuge and wasn't surprised who she found. "Joyce?"

"I'm not feeling well, love," she said. She coughed into her blood-soaked handkerchief.

Sister Sue shook her head. "You should be in hospital."

"No. I want to be here when Sam gets back." But she sank to the floor, unable to stand anymore, and Sue raced to call an ambulance.

With much sadness, Sue contemplated the worst. She and Joyce had been friends since their teens. They had studied together in Rome, lived with each other for years and had also been bridesmaids at each other's weddings. Marrying two brothers had made them real family.

Raising their children together while travelling with their husbands all over Europe had been an exciting time for them both. It had been the happiest period of their lives, until the accident that had taken both their children and husbands away from them.

The memory of the car crash, almost twenty years ago, was still clear in Sue's mind.

Watching Joyce being carried out to the ambulance brought back everything about that tragic day. Her faith in God had kept her going all these years, and she knew he would continue to help her one day at a time.

She had also looked to God for understanding as to why Joyce didn't want Sam to find out about who they really were and how much they loved her. But she would never betray Joyce and therefore, couldn't tell Sam anything about their shared history. It had saddened her to have kept quiet all these years, but her reward was spending the last five years with Sam and that was worth it.

She picked up the phone and dialled her second in charge, forgetting Jenny was in Melbourne on training. She stopped the first sister who walked past her office. "Sister Jan, come in, please. Tonight, you are my 2IC as I'm off to the hospital to see Joyce. If there are any problems, call me on my mobile. I'll be back as soon as I can."

———

St Vincent's Hospital's emergency desk was jam-packed with patients and their family members and Sue knew she didn't have time to waste, so she slipped through the crowd and into the emergency room without anyone noticing.

The row of ambulance gurneys with patients on them waiting for attention was distressing for her but she kept on searching for her friend. Overwhelmed at the sight and sounds of so many suffering people, she burst into tears.

As she stood in the middle of the emergency room weeping,

a kind voice spoke from behind her. "Excuse me, Sister, can I help you? Are you looking for someone?"

She swiftly wiped her eyes with her hands and turned around to see a tall dark-haired young doctor holding a folder and looking concerned. "Yes, please. I'm looking for Joyce Thomas. The ambulance brought her here."

"Hello, I'm Dr Yasi. I was here when Joyce came in and I'm sorry to say her condition is critical, and she was transferred to intensive care. You may go in and see her, but I must prepare you for what you will find.

"Her lungs are shutting down and her body is not getting the oxygen it needs. There is nothing we can do but try to make her comfortable. I'm sorry, but it's only a matter of time now." He directed her to where she could find Joyce.

Sister Sue put on her best face and walked into the intensive care unit with a smile. She was devastated to see Joyce strapped up to the oxygen apparatus next to her bed. Her friend's face was pale, her cheeks sallow and dark rings had formed under her eyes. Her blue lips were clearly visible through the face mask.

Hearing her enter, Joyce opened her eyes, ripped off the mask and tears streamed down her face. "You took your time." She struggled with each word.

"Did you wait for me?" Sue said with a smile, holding back her heartbreak.

Joyce struggled through the words. "I don't want Sam to see me like this," she said, breathing heavily with short, shallow gusts of air.

This tore Sue's heart out and she reached out to take her hand and mustered all the strength she could to hold back her tears. "She won't, my darling."

"I'm ready to see my little Nicole now," Joyce whispered.

"I know, honey, I know." She blinked back the tears.

"I love you, Sue," Joyce mumbled. Then all the bells and alarms sounded at the same time.

A nurse came in and led Sue to a chair as she cried out Joyce's name. Another nurse appeared and checked Joyce's vitals, then systematically turned off each of the alarms and monitors.

"She's gone," the nurse said. "Would you like to stay for a while and say goodbye?"

Sue had expected this but still wasn't ready for it and sank back into the chair and wept.

AUSTRALIAN MUSEUM

The shortcut through Hyde Park got Sam to the museum in no time at all and, with a deep breath, she walked through the grand entrance.

"Welcome to the Australian Museum. The line for tickets is to your left. Have a nice day," said an elderly man in a sharp black suit with a red bowtie, before turning to usher in a group of school children.

"Excuse me, sir, can you direct me to Mr Charles Harman, please?" Sam asked, showing him the business card.

"Who, may I ask, is here to see him?" he asked politely.

"My name is Samantha Page."

"Yes ma'am, certainly. I am James Barlow. Please follow me, I will escort you to his office." With a wave of one hand, he directed his younger assistant to take his place at the door.

Sam couldn't believe her ears. No one had ever spoken to her like that before and it felt good.

The walk was long, and her anticipation grew at every twist and turn James took. The hallway they travelled along was behind the exhibitions and displays, and the many 'staff only' signs along the way showed it was not for public use.

There were various workrooms, and she was dying to take a quick peek at all the behind-the-scenes activities, with historic artefacts and half-finished displays being worked on by an array of people in crisp white lab coats.

The office door, at the end of the last corridor, was open, but James stopped at the doorway and waited until the person in the office had finished his call.

"Excuse me, sir, I have a Samantha Page here to see you," James announced, standing almost at attention, his back ramrod straight and arms at his sides.

"Thank you, James. Please send her in," a male voice said.

"It was a pleasure to meet you, Samantha. You may go in. Mr Harman will see you now." Stepping to one side, James waited until Sam walked into the office before closing the door behind her.

Sam entered slowly and felt as if she had stepped onto the bridge of a ship. The spectacular panoramic views overlooking Hyde Park took her breath away, but the artefact and photographic collection that filled the office was even more remarkable. She couldn't believe it was an office and didn't know where to look first.

"Please come in. Take a seat. I'm Charles Harman, Director and CEO of the Australian Museum. Tell me, do we have an appointment?" he asked while looking at his open desk diary.

"No, sir. Joyce Thomas sent me to see you about a job. She said you were looking for people and for me to get in early before all the jobs are filled," Sam explained, trying hard not to look away from him.

"Yes, I planned to start a new round of recruitment as of tomorrow, but who sent you again?" he asked, looking puzzled.

"Joyce Thomas. She gave me this card, sir." Sam handed it to him.

"That's my business card all right," he said with a smile and returned it. "Please describe her to me."

"She's a lovely old grey-haired lady who I only met today. She's a little shorter than me and doesn't look well; a little frail even. But she was very pushy about me coming to see you right away."

"Did she perhaps have very dark brown eyes?"

"Yes. I could never forget those eyes."

"Oh, that's Joyce Page, she was on the board of the museum. She was our chairperson for a time."

Time stopped for Sam. Her heart started beating fast. "What did you say her name was?"

"Joyce Page. Is she any relation?"

"That's what I'm wondering. I only met her today."

"You know, Joyce had the final say in hiring me for this position. I've been here five years now and I've been so very grateful to her giving me this opportunity. Unfortunately, soon after I took up the position, she stepped down from the board, and we haven't stayed in touch. Whatever the situation, a relative or not, if she sent you here then that's good enough for me," he said as he retrieved a folder with 'recruitment' written on the front.

"Now, we have five positions available. Two lab assistant roles, two ticketing staff roles and one ticketing manager role. The lab roles are mainly cleaning duties so let's put you in a ticketing staff position. What do you say about that?"

"I would prefer one of the lab assistant roles if you don't mind, sir," she said, holding her breath in hope. Words and numbers terrified her, so cleaning was her best option.

"If you prefer to work in the lab, then congratulations and welcome aboard. Let's start you next Monday, a week from now. Your staff induction will commence then, so be here by 8:30 a.m. You will report to your laboratory manager, Tom Anderson, who will go through all your necessary paperwork before you start the staff induction. Please direct any questions to him. How's that?"

Sam nodded in agreement.

"And I would be very grateful if you would inform Joyce of this and pass on my regards next time you see her."

Mr Harman personally escorted Samantha back to the front entrance and entertained her with fascinating stories of some of the exhibitions they came across along the way. Sam appreciated the effort and the job, but her mind was occupied trying to understand who Joyce Page was and why she had introduced herself as Joyce Thomas.

As soon as they reached the front entrance, she thanked Mr Harman for his time. After giving him a firm handshake, she raced back to the refuge, hoping Joyce was still there.

———

"Sister Sue, Sister Sue, earlier today just before lunch, you came into the toilets and found me and an old lady in there, do you remember?" Sam asked as she burst into the sister's office.

"Yes, of course I remember," Sister Sue replied.

"I'm looking for the old lady. Do you know where she is?"

The woman's face fell, her eyes filling with tears as she reached out her hands to take Sam's. "Yes, I'm sorry to say she collapsed, and we called an ambulance. But they couldn't help her, the poor old thing. She died. God bless her."

Sam couldn't believe what she was hearing. "Where did they take her?"

"St Vincent Hospital but—"

Sam ran from the room and raced to the hospital, only a

few blocks away. But they only confirmed Sister Sue's story. Joyce had died of suspected heart failure.

Sam didn't know why she felt the way she did. After all, she hardly knew the woman. But where had she come from and why had she made the effort to talk to her?

She thought back to her interview at the museum. At least she finally had a job! Earning a regular wage and enjoying some sort of reasonable existence was now a real possibility.

Tears of happiness filled her eyes. But it was bittersweet because her thoughts immediately returned to Joyce. Who was she? Why did she have the same surname? And why had she come into her life now, only to leave with so many unanswered questions?

The refuge would be her best chance of finding someone who knew Joyce. She was determined to leave no stone unturned to discover all she could about the mysterious Joyce Thomas Page.

THE JOB

The week flew by and by the end of it, Sam was exhausted. Anyone she came across at the shelter was subject to a barrage of questions about Joyce. Yet still, she had no answers. No one knew her or had even heard of her.

Maybe she wasn't real. But she still had the business card in her pocket, so she quickly dismissed that notion.

Sunday night arrived, and as she prepared her clothes to wear to her first day of work, a peace settled over her when she realised she could ask Mr Harman about Joyce.

Sam got up extra early, put on an old dress and covered her hair with a blue and yellow scarf, then took off to help with breakfast at the refuge. It was more crowded than usual so preparing and serving the food was hard work. But it helped to settle her nerves.

At seven-fifteen, a few sisters got together to remind her to start getting ready for her new job at the museum. They all held hands and ran around in a circle with her in the middle shouting, "New job! New job!"

They sent her off home where she had a quick shower, got

dressed and carefully applied the red lipstick she had squir-relled away for this day. She walked briskly across Hyde Park and slowed down further as she approached the museum.

Arriving with five minutes to spare, Sam was led into the staff room and told to wait there. She didn't need to wait long.

"Hi, Samantha. I'm Tom Anderson, the laboratory manager." He offered his hand and gave her a firm handshake.

"Hi, Tom," she said, returning his friendly smile.

"About our dress code—you can arrive and leave dressed however you want but you will be issued daily with a special set of work overalls that don't leave the museum. It's our responsibility to clean and maintain them, you understand." Without waiting for her acknowledgment, he continued, "Please come with me to the laboratory where we can sort out your paperwork and start on your induction. You'll be an old hand in no time." Tom chuckled as he kept one eye on Sam while escorting her down deep into the pits of the museum.

She kept sneaking looks at him. He was stunning. He stood over six feet tall, had brilliant blue eyes, a fair complexion and shoulder-length wavy blonde hair tied back in a ponytail. She guessed he was in his early thirties and she loved his gorgeous smile. His clothes looked as if they'd come out of the same charity donation bin as hers, but she couldn't keep her eyes off his brawny arms and shoulders. It wasn't until they were almost finished filling out the paperwork that she noticed he wore a wedding ring.

The room they were in was completely enclosed by four enormous laboratories, separated from them by ten-inch-thick multi-layer glass walls. Sam was told she could only enter this room using the elevator and that the entrance to any of the laboratories was only via this room, but only after completing some sort of sterilisation routine. It was all too much for her to understand so she just held on for the ride.

"Before we commence your staff induction, first let's get to know a little about each other, I'll go first. I've been married ten years, and I've got two kids—Jenny is eight and Tom Junior is seven. My wife Sue works in a bank and we live in Redfern.

"It's hard to believe, but I've been here for almost fifteen years and I've had the laboratory manager position for about five years. You know, I started here in the very same position you are in. Anyway, enough of me, tell me about you," Tom said as he politely pointed at her with a smile.

Before Sam could run, Bruce grabbed her by the hair with one hand and forced her into her bedroom. Leaving the door open, he king-hit her so hard she fell face-down on the bed as Sam sobbed. "I'm telling Grandma and Poppy how you treat me. I'm telling them how you come into my room at night. I'm telling them everything!"

Sam pushed the memories of her foster father out of her mind. She hated it when they arose and took over everything. They were in the past, and now she had a job, something Bruce had told her would never happen. "I grew up in Melbourne and moved here when I was eighteen." *Thanks to the help of the government youth protection assistance programme, but he doesn't need to know that.* "I've been trying to find a job for a while now and have been volunteering at a local women's refuge to get some work experience. The sisters there were so good to help me out."

She asked Tom if he knew Joyce Thomas. But Tom made it clear he had nothing to do with senior management, especially the board of directors. He put on a serious face. "Look, you are not getting any special treatment from me just because the boss hired you. If you don't pull your weight around here or if you get here late, you're out!" Then, with a ghost of a smile, he shook his finger at her. "And don't even think about chucking a sick day, okay?"

With a short burst of laughter, Sam shook her head from side to side. "No way." She loved everything about him and knew she would love working with him. He made her feel comfortable in every way.

"Do you have any questions, Sam?"

"If we are in here doing this, who is doing the cleaning?"

"We have contract cleaners. We are the only permanent cleaning staff and it's my job to coordinate the contract cleaning crews. Your job is more about touching up their work after they complete a big job."

Tom began breaking down her duties clearly and systematically. Cleaning was her main function and anything else was left to the other staff. He drummed this into her for hours and explained they used specially formulated cleaning detergents rather than supermarket brands to avoid damaging the fossils, artefacts, and other delicate items.

Tom gave her a comprehensive cleaning demonstration and Sam was enthralled.

"Okay, let's break for lunch. I bring my own sandwiches and eat them in the park across the road. You can join me if you like."

Sam didn't know what to say and kept packing away the cleaning equipment he had used for his demonstration.

"I get it—you want to be alone. No worries. Let's meet in the lobby after lunch. You haven't got an electronic pass yet, so I will organise one for you to allow you to access the lab without calling me. You have one hour for lunch, so I'll see you in an hour." He smiled, grabbed his lunch, and walked her out to the foyer.

It was a beautiful sunny day. Sam gave Tom a little wave and headed for the refuge. It was lunchtime and she didn't want to miss out. In her excitement, she had forgotten to eat breakfast and was starving. Her legs were shaking, and she felt faint, so she paused for a minute or two to muster her strength before continuing on her way.

Somehow, she made it to the refuge and thankfully accepted a glass of orange juice from Sister Sue, who pestered her with questions about her new job. But Sam was ravenous and before she could reply, she munched through an assortment of meat and salad sandwiches washed down with more orange juice.

Once satisfied, she was back on her feet, feeling grateful for Sue's kindness, but Sam knew the nun had always been appreciative of her tireless generosity in helping out at the refuge over the last five years.

Realising her lunch hour was nearly over, she said goodbye to Sister Sue, grabbed a couple of bananas and an apple and took off like the wind, back to the museum.

"Hello, Sam. How are you enjoying your new job?" Mr Harman asked, startling her from behind as she walked into the foyer.

"Yes, very much, thank you," she replied, and, with a deep breath, she looked into his hazel green eyes. "Mr Harman, can I bother you with a question?"

"Yes, of course, go ahead." He walked her to a quiet area at the front of the foyer.

"It's about Joyce Thomas. You referred to her as Joyce Page. Can you tell me a little more about her, please? Anything would be helpful."

"First of all, I hope you had the opportunity to tell her about me hiring you?"

"No, I didn't, I'm sorry. That same day she collapsed, and an ambulance took her to St Vincent Hospital. After my interview, I raced over there but they told me she had died." Sam was steadfast in showing no emotion after seeing Mr Harman's eyes start to tear up.

"I'm so sorry to hear this. My sincere condolences. Let's go to my office." He put one arm around her and started walking. He stopped for a moment and whispered to James, "Please inform Tom that Sam is with me and I will send her down once we are finished."

"Yes, sir," James replied.

Sam's silent heartbreak had subsided by the time they got to his office. She placed her bag on the seat next to her and drank the glass of water Mr Harman kindly poured for her.

Then he sighed and sat down heavily at his desk, folding his hands in front of them. "Apart from the two job interviews, Joyce and I never met. She stepped down from her board position soon after I started so I never had the chance to tell her how thankful I was for her confidence in me. It was after resigning from the board that she started using her maiden name of Thomas, I believe."

When Sam heard all this, her heart sank. Would she ever know the truth about the mysterious Joyce? She thanked Mr Harman for his kindness and went back to the lab to continue her training.

THE BOOK GLASSES

After a week of training one-on-one with Tom, Sam commenced her duties. Working on the small exhibitions and cleaning up the day-to-day spills children would make during their visit took up most of her time.

The contract cleaners worked the night shift, leaving Tom and Sam to take care of all the small jobs and the general spills and mess left behind by museum visitors during the day.

Seeing the magnificent exhibitions every day was never boring. The more she saw them, the more excited she was about them. Each day she noticed something new. As the days passed, Sam would pinch herself to make sure she wasn't dreaming because everything was perfect. The staff were always polite and kind to her, the building was spectacular, and she loved the museum's wonderful exhibitions.

But it was the work she loved the most. It didn't require her to read and, for the first time, she was free from the embarrassment of feeling useless and dumb. Now that she was earning a regular weekly wage, she was able to start a new life and hoped to meet someone special. For the first time in her life, things were exciting for her and joy was slowly entering her life. It was strange at first, but she felt she was ready for it.

Just after opening time, Sam was attending to a mishap in between Mesozoic World and the T-Rex exhibitions when she was knocked to the floor by a group of three men running down the hallway swearing and screaming at each other. She didn't get a good look at them but when she got up and dusted herself off, she realised they had come out of Mr Harman's office.

Dropping what she was doing, she ran to his office. She couldn't believe her eyes. It was trashed—everything was on the floor. Even the huge solid oak desk was lying on its side.

She called out to Mr Harman and heard his muted reply from under his desk.

"Mr Harman, are you alright?" Sam asked and then screamed upon seeing he was pinned under his desk with a knife protruding from his chest. Sam noticed his lips were turning blue and started to panic.

"I've pressed the silent alarm, Sam, and security will be here very soon, so I would like you to listen to me very carefully. I need you to open the bottom drawer of my desk and remove the false bottom. There, you will find a glasses case, in which you will find a set of odd-looking reading glasses. I would like you to take the case and do not, under any circumstances, tell anyone you have it. Are you listening, Sam?' Then with a strong voice he said, "Go, do it now!"

She could hardly see through her teary eyes but finally managed to locate the glasses. "Mr Harman, I—"

But it was too late. He was gone. She screamed even louder.

"Step aside ma'am. Security here!" commanded a tall dark man in a uniform displaying the museum's logo on the shirt pocket.

Before she knew it, there were half a dozen security guards

crowded into the office. It seemed as if they were all talking at once, whether into the two-way radios they all wore or to each other. The first guard escorted her out of the office and told her to wait nearby until the police arrived.

She was shaking like a leaf. Why would anyone do this to Mr Harman? Who would want to hurt such a kind and gentle man? She collapsed into a chair and held her head in her hands.

The police soon came—first a couple of uniformed officers, then a handful of detectives and eventually, it seemed as if half of the forensic department was there. It wasn't enough that they interrogated Sam outside Mr Harman's office, they asked her to go with them to the police station to make a full statement, explaining to her that it was best to do so immediately after the event.

Sam didn't argue after Tom encouraged her to go with them, for Mr Harman's sake. She went, not realising she still held the glasses case in her hands.

At the police station, they escorted her into an interview room and asked her to walk them through what had happened. Then they peppered her with questions and their interrogative style was exhausting.

Finally, the formal interview was over. For a moment she just stared at the huge mirror on the opposite wall, totally numb.

"Thank you for your statement, Samantha. Please sign here and I can drive you back to work. You can use your glasses to read your statement before you sign it if you like?" the detective said, pointing at the glasses case she was still clutching in her hands.

The glasses case, she screamed silently to herself. *I still have it!* A cold shiver ran up and down her body. She hadn't mentioned it in her statement. She'd forgotten that she'd been holding in her hands the whole time.

"No, I don't need them to read, thank you," she replied with a quiver in her voice. She knew how to scribble her name, but she wasn't going to reveal she couldn't read. And now she couldn't even use the excuse that she needed reading glasses.

"Are you all right, love?" the detective asked, noticing her distress.

"I'm fine, thank you. It's all been a bit much for me, that's all. I'll be okay," she responded convincingly. After pretending to carefully read the statement, she signed her name at the bottom.

Sam shivered in the back of the police car all the way back to the museum. On her arrival, she calmly got out of the car and managed to make her way to the staff room without anyone noticing she was back.

The room was empty, so she sat down and stared at the glasses case. It was time to find out what was inside.

She slowly opened it and was a little disappointed to find a pair of old-style reading glasses resting on a note. But when she heard the staff room door open, she quickly closed the glasses case. It made a loud snapping sound that seemed to echo around the room.

One of the security guards entered and Sam held her breath until he passed her with a brief nod and started to make a cup of tea. She stowed the case in her locker, under her handbag, and headed back to the laboratory.

"Hi, Sam. I heard what happened to poor Mr Harman. Are you all right?" asked one of the ticketing staff as she walked down the hallway towards her.

"I was told by the police not to discuss it with anyone, sorry, so I can't say anything about it. I've got to go back to work now, bye," Sam said and continued on her way.

She couldn't stop thinking about the reading glasses and the note resting underneath them. She knew she wouldn't be able to read it. Yet, giving it to someone else was out of the question. After all, Mr Harman had expressly instructed her to not tell anyone she had the glasses. What should she do?

When she bumped into Tom in the elevator, she habitually held back all emotions.

"Sam, what are you doing here? Go home!" Tom said with a tremor in his voice while he hugged her tightly.

He led her back up to the staff room, waited until she retrieved her gear from her locker and walked her out to the front of the museum. He explained to her that once she got some counselling and other proper support, then and only then, would she be allowed back to work. He also clearly stated that she would be on leave, with full pay, until she was ready to return to work. "Don't worry about anything here. Are you sure you're okay to get yourself home?"

Sam nodded and Tom gave her another hug and waved goodbye. She walked out the front doors without looking back.

Unable to face her empty apartment, Sam headed for the refuge. When she couldn't find Sister Sue, she made her way to the kitchen and found some sandwiches left over from lunch. She had almost polished off a plateful when someone approached her from behind.

"Get out of my kitchen. You've got money now!" cried Sister Sue, who laughed when Sam spat out what was left in her mouth in fright.

"Hey, you scared me. I nearly choked!" she yelled, astonishing her.

"What's wrong?" she asked.

Through her coughing, Sam told her what had happened, leaving out the bit about the glasses. Sister Sue wrapped her arms around her and held her like a mother would hold her child. "Tom is right," she said, "You should go home and rest. Anytime you need support, I'll be here. Just drop in."

After receiving another hug from Sue, she picked up her bag and headed home.

―――――

Hours later, alone in her apartment, Sam retrieved the glasses case from her bag and opened it. She took the glasses out of the case, placed them on the kitchen table and unfolded the note. To Sam, it may as well have been hieroglyphics. In frustration, she tossed it across the table.

Feeling sorry for herself, she picked up the glasses and studied them. They were heavy; the frames were made from steel. And the lenses were so clear that it looked like there was nothing in the frames at all. They were covered in unusual symbols and engravings. Without another thought, she put them on.

A rush of adrenaline surged throughout her body. To steady herself, she closed her eyes and placed both hands on the table, palms down.

Upon opening her eyes, the first thing she saw was the note she had tossed onto the table. She was amazed to see that the hieroglyphics had miraculously turned into words. Even more astonishing, she could understand them!

COMMISSIONED BY THE PAPAL BASILICA OF ST PETER, VATICAN CITY 1758.

TO MY SUCCESSORS, YOUR EMINENCE, I PRESENT TO YOU THE BOOK GLASSES. THROUGH THEIR POWER AND THAT OF THE HOLY SPIRIT, MAY THE CHURCH BE TRULY RENEWED. WE PUT OUR HOPE IN THE LORD, THAT HE WILL ASSIST US AND GUIDE US. LET US GO FORWARD WITH

THE LORD IN THE CERTAINTY THAT THE LORD
WILL CONQUER.
   HIS HOLINESS POPE BENEDICT XIV

"*What just happened?!*" Sam screamed. She took off the glasses, placed them on the table and moved back as if they were deadly.

Rising from her single dining room chair that didn't match the dining room table, she started pacing back and forth across her apartment. After several minutes, she sat back down in the worn chair and looked at the note. The writing was back to hieroglyphics.

What is going on?

She glanced at the glasses and back at the note, alternating between the two for a while, before building up enough courage to put the glasses back on.

As soon as she did, the hieroglyphics turned into words and she was again able to effortlessly read the note. She took the glasses off, folded the note, and placed it back in the case along with the glasses.

"I can read! I can read!" she said, filled with joy and wonder. But then she realised that it was not her but the glasses. Her newfound happiness turned into confusion.

She pictured Mr Harman lying on the floor of his office covered in blood, instructing her to tell no one she had them. She couldn't leave them on the table for anyone to find so she picked up the case and hid it under a loose floorboard in the bottom of her almost empty bedroom closet. It was the best place she could think of.

Then she lay down on her bed and tried to figure out how she could read while wearing the glasses. The note referred to them as the book glasses. She had understood every word written by some pope in 1758, addressed to all future popes.

She couldn't believe she had understood it. It was incredible. She fell asleep thinking about it without even changing into her pyjamas or brushing her teeth.

A PARCEL

Sam woke the next morning with a start as the sun peeked over the horizon.

After a quick shower, she dressed and set off for her routine volunteering duties—serving breakfast at the refuge. She raced like the wind to arrive in the kitchen and have everything set up before the sisters got there but she was surprised to find Sister Sue barring her way, a rolling pin in one hand.

"Oh no you don't. You are not helping out today, young lady. Off you go back home and I don't want to see you all week." she said.

"What are you going to do with that?" Sam asked and laughed.

"You take another step in and I'll show you what I'll do with it. Now, go on, get out of here!" Sister Sue wasn't joking. It was strange for Sam to see her like this.

Disappointed she couldn't help, she grabbed a few bananas and apples and a handful of grapes from the kitchen bench and turned around to head back home.

When she arrived back at her apartment she went back to

bed. She soon fell asleep, wondering what she would do with her free time.

By the time the doorbell rang and woke her, it was almost lunchtime. She hurriedly jumped out of bed and opened the door. Disappointed to discover no one there, she noticed a parcel on the floor.

After looking up and down the corridor, she picked it up and took it inside, making sure to lock the door behind her.

She couldn't read the address, so she ripped open the huge yellow envelope, reached in and pulled out a book. For a while, she just stared at it and then flipped through it, but there wasn't a single picture or anything else to help her determine what it was about. She shoved the book back in the yellow envelope and threw it across the room in frustration.

Nearly an hour later, as she was washing up her cup and plate after lunch, she decided to use the glasses to find out what the book was about. She dried her hands and retrieved the parcel and the book glasses and placed them in front of her on the kitchen table.

With a deep breath, she pulled out the book, opened it and put on the glasses.

It was like déjà vu. She could read!

The parcel was addressed to her next-door neighbour and the book was called *Principles of Administrative Law*. It was the Second Edition by Peter Cane and Leighton McDonald, 15th July 2013.

She turned it over and was able to read the text on the back cover effortlessly:

This book provides a clear and concise account of the main principles of administrative law. More than that, it sets those principles in historical, comparative, and constitutional perspective. Principles of Administrative Law *guides the reader through the complexities of the current law and provides an account of how it developed and where it might go in the years to come. This book tells not only what administrative law is but also what it is about. It explains as well as informs...*

Once she had read to the bottom of the page, she took off the glasses with disbelief and astonishment. Not only could she read the words, but she could also understand what they meant.

After contemplating whether to take the textbook to her neighbours, she opened it and began reading from the start. One page turned into two, then ten and twenty. In twenty minutes, she was halfway through the four-hundred-page book.

She took off the glasses, gently placed them on the table and paced around the apartment, trying to work out what had just happened. It wasn't only the speed reading that shook her up, it was the fact she understood the contents and retained the knowledge. It was astonishing.

Hungry for more, she sat down, put on the glasses again and picked up the book. Twenty minutes later, she had finished reading it and had verified it wasn't a one-off incident—it was the book glasses.

She returned the glasses to their case and put it back in its hiding spot. At a loss of what to do next, she decided to go for a walk. Walking was always helpful when she had something to figure out. Once she'd returned to her apartment after taking the law textbook next door, Sam changed her clothes and headed out of the building.

She walked for many blocks. On her way home, with her new-found self-confidence, she located an automatic teller and did something she had never done before—withdrew money for herself. After taking out one hundred dollars, she carefully put it away and hurried home.

Although excited about her achievement, things were no

better for her once she was back in her apartment. She still did not know what to do about the book glasses.

When she took the money out and placed it on the table, tears started streaming down her cheeks. They were a mixture of happy tears because she finally had some money of her own and proud tears as she had used an automatic teller by herself, but mostly sad tears as she mourned the loss of Joyce and Mr Harman, two people she barely knew.

Then, with a new sense of excitement, she contemplated pushing things further with the book glasses to test their limits. There were no books in her apartment, so she ran over to the refuge and grabbed a handful from the library without anyone noticing.

She tossed the books onto the kitchen table and retrieved the glasses. She put them on and started reading the titles and authors: *Moby-Dick* by Herman Melville; *The Color Purple* by Alice Walker; *Schindler's List* by Thomas Keneally; *Pride and Prejudice* by Jane Austen; *Misery* by Stephen King and *Australian School's Oxford Dictionary Fourth Edition*.

Awestruck that she could read each book's title and author name, she dared herself to read them all.

She picked up *Moby-Dick* and began to read. The speed at which she read was astonishing but what blew her away was how she understood the meaning of every word; somehow, she knew that even her pronunciation was faultless.

Once she'd finished the last of the five books, she came up with an idea to further test the glasses.

Starting with *Moby-Dick*, she selected six unusual words from the novel and wrote them down on a note pad. To her amazement, she then wrote out the definition of each word with ease; almost verbatim dictionary descriptions after checking.

Vain—showing an excessively high opinion of one's appearance, abilities or worth.

Tribulation—a state of great trouble or suffering.

Leviathan—monstrous sea creature symbolising evil in the Old Testament.

Zephyr—a slight wind.

Supplicate—ask for humbly or earnestly, as in prayer.

Inexorable—impervious to pleas, persuasion, requests, reason.

"How is this possible?" she asked the empty room and sat back in her chair, scratching her head.

She took off the glasses and her dyslexia was back; she couldn't even read the book covers, let alone understand the words on the pages.

She donned the glasses and picked up *The Color Purple*, opened it and selected six more words.

Crib—baby bed.

Fornication—sexual intercourse between persons not married to each other.

Pomade—hairdressing consisting of a perfumed oil or ointment.

Primp—dress or groom with elaborate care.

Strumpet—a woman adulterer.

Sass—answer back in an impudent or insolent manner.

After laying *The Color Purple* back on the table, she chose *Schindler's List* and again selected some words.

Genocide—the deliberate and total extermination of a culture.

Ghetto—poor sections of cities.

Gypsies—wandering people, originally from India.

Holocaust—systematic and bureaucratic annihilation of millions of people.

Resistance—acts of rebellion, sabotage and attempts to

escape.

Racism—The belief that a racial group is inferior because of biological or cultural traits.

She realised these were serious words and thought back over the story she had read about the Holocaust in which so many innocent people had died and how Schindler had worked to save the people on his list. Despite reading the book so quickly, she could recall the full story in great detail.

From *Pride and Prejudice*, she selected another six words:

Scrupulous—characterised by extreme care and great effort.

Vex—disturb, especially by minor irritations.

Supercilious—having or showing arrogant disdain or haughtiness.

Impertinent—improperly forward or bold.

Persevere—be persistent, refuse to stop.

Indifference—the trait of remaining calm and seeming not to care.

Sam studied the worn cover of *Pride and Prejudice* and imagined living the life of the story's heroine, Elizabeth Bennet. How different would it have been to grow up in a big house in the country with a mother and father and sisters, and to wear fancy dresses like the woman on the cover and dance at balls with handsome gentlemen?

After returning to the present day, she put the book down and selected half a dozen words from the last book, *Misery*.

Carnivorous—relating to flesh-eating animals.

Malevolence—wishing evil to others.

Paradox—a statement that contradicts itself.

Sinister—wicked, evil, or dishonourable.

Deteriorate—become worse or disintegrate.

Alter ego—a very close friend who seems almost a part of yourself.

Once finished, Sam didn't need to check to see if her

answers were correct; she intuitively knew they were all one hundred percent accurate. The sudden ability to break down and understand complex words, words she previously would never have imagined, was effortless.

Her experiment had worked, and she was thrilled beyond belief. For the first time in her life, she could read books. Dreaming of endless possibilities, she picked up all the books and cradled them in her arms, dancing around the apartment with them.

She had triumphed over her disability. She had been given a gift from God and had accepted it with fortitude and gratefulness. Now, nothing could stop her from reading as many books as she could.

Her stomach rumbled and she realised she had forgotten to eat. She stowed the books in a plastic bag and planned to drop them back at the refuge on her way to get something to eat at the local shops. The thought of daring to venture into the shops was exhilarating.

After again hiding away the glasses, she scooped up the money from the kitchen table along with the bag of books and headed for the refuge.

THE LIBRARY

Sam had always enjoyed walking in the dark, secure in her anonymity, with fewer people on the streets for her to avoid. She hated people looking at her, feeling they could somehow see she was stupid and couldn't read.

Not anymore, she told herself.

This time she was overflowing with confidence. It skyrocketed as she realised she had strategised her route for maximum efficiency, unconsciously calculating times and distances, even taking into account weather conditions like wind velocity and humidity. Also, she was unusually aware of her surroundings.

It was clear to her that the book glasses were responsible for her newfound good fortune and, with every discovery, it was more difficult for her to contemplate doing anything without them.

The following morning, she woke with a start, feeling the need to prepare for her ten-day series of counselling sessions; a requirement before she could go back to work. After her morning muesli, she took off to the library to research what to expect.

On her arrival, the woman at the front desk asked for her name and contact details before allowing her to borrow a book, so she slipped on the book glasses and proudly filled in her details on the woman's iPad. Her confidence glowed brighter than the sun.

Then she located the counselling section and selected the first book she found: *Controlling Stress and Tension* by Daniel Girdano, Dorothy E Dusel and George S Everly Jr.

Settled in an armchair in the middle of the library in front of everyone, Sam read the book from cover to cover. Her fear and self-consciousness evaporated, and her defences were demolished. It was liberating. The book helped her to understand her feelings and taught her strategies to keep stress and tension in check and better cope with the death of Mr Harman. She was now ready to discuss the incident with a counsellor.

But there was one thing she would not mention.

As she put the book back on the shelf, she scanned the others. There were so many and so much to know. But she wouldn't need to visit the library every day to access information if she had a computer.

Excited about the endless possibilities she could discover over the internet, she strode out of the Sydney City Library. Her excitement grew at the thought of the adventures in learning ahead of her, both online and via physical books. She felt free from limitations and ready to move forward into the future. The library had always represented the future for Sam and she truly believed she had an exciting one ahead.

REMEMBRANCE

Sister Sue looked around the refuge's meal hall.

Sam wasn't there again. She had never been absent for so long before. Since she had started volunteering, she had never stayed away longer than one or two days. Like clockwork, she would be there for breakfast, lunch, and dinner, helping before she would ever help herself. Even if she was going for a job interview or temporarily had a job, she would still drop in for part of the day.

The fact that Sam had been away so long, especially over Christmas, was strange and Sister Sue was determined to find out what was keeping her away.

She couldn't lose her. She couldn't live without her. Especially not now Joyce had gone as well.

"Sue Page, you bring those smokes back to me right now, or so help me, I'll tell your husband all about those men you've had," Joyce shouted.

Sue laughed. "Go ahead. He'll never believe you."

"Come on, stop it and give me my bloody smokes back, you

cow." Joyce folded her arms across her chest and pouted at her friend.

"Here you go. If you get cancer don't come crying to me." Sue hurled the pack of Twenty-fives across the kitchen to her.

"I wish you would stop doing that. You're not helping," Joyce said, lighting up a cigarette.

"Don't smoke in here, you cow. Get out." Sue raced for the phone as it started ringing.

As the voice buzzed on the other end of the line, Sue's blood froze. She couldn't be hearing this. No! It wasn't possible!

She put the phone down and screamed and screamed.

Joyce raced back inside. "What's wrong?"

It took a while for Sue to calm down enough to explain it was the Royal Melbourne Hospital calling to say that both their husbands had been in a serious car accident.

The two women held each other, screaming and crying in fear and disbelief.

"What about Samantha and Nicole?" Joyce asked.

"They didn't say anything about our babies. Come on, we need to be strong for them. I'll drive." After handing Joyce some tissues, Sue wiped her eyes and mustered enough courage to get them both into the car and to the hospital.

At the emergency desk, they enquired about their husbands and were ushered into a small office. A man entered and introduced himself as Dr Amal Michaeal. He informed them that both men had been pronounced dead on arrival at the hospital as a result of the severe injuries they had sustained in the accident.

"What about our girls, Samantha and Nicole? Where are our baby girls?" Sue asked.

"According to the ambulance officers, there was only one girl in the car and I'm sorry to inform you she was pronounced dead on arrival," said the doctor.

"But they were going to pick up my daughter Samantha

from my in-laws. I need to ring them now," Sue shouted in a panic.

"Here, please use my phone." The doctor pointed to the phone on his desk.

Sue dialled the number and was overwhelmed with relief to hear that Samantha was there, safe and sound. But then she had to tell her in-laws that their sons, along with baby Nicole, were dead.

It was too much to bear. How would they cope without their husbands? And little Nicole, gone forever. She looked over to the chair where Joyce sat weeping and joined her.

So many tragedies, so many mistakes. She couldn't make another one, not again, not with Sam. Sue needed to get her back.

THE PROFESSOR

The ten days of counselling were finally over, and Sam had found the process helpful, despite her preoccupation with books. She had immersed herself in reading and learning to the exclusion of almost everything else.

A few days later, she received a letter of notice from the museum, requesting her to return to work. But reluctance gnawed at her. How could she go back to doing manual labour?

She got dressed and headed in the next day after her usual bowl of muesli. She took the book glasses with her in her handbag. When she arrived, she wore a gloomy face for all to notice.

"Morning, Samantha. It's good to see you back, my dear," said James with a genuine smile before hurrying past her to help a customer with an enquiry.

"Hi, James," Sam replied with a serious frown and went to find Tom. It was time to hand in her notice. Now she had the glasses she knew they'd help her get a better job.

As she stepped out of the elevator, Tom rushed past her. "Hi, Sam, thanks for coming in. I'm glad to see you. I'm under the pump today and I need you out in the foyer area now, please. We've just had a spill. I've got a problem at the delivery docks and I need to go, but let's catch up at lunchtime."

The lift doors closed before Sam had a chance to respond so she shrugged and changed into her work overalls.

By the time she arrived in the foyer, it was mayhem. Although the ticketing staff had already placed "slippery when wet" signs at key locations, they were being ignored and there were not enough staff to keep unobservant visitors, especially children, away from the spills.

Children were crying and parents and teachers were taking out their frustration and anger on poor James, yelling and screaming at him because some of the children had slipped after spilling their drinks while waiting to go into the museum. Sam cleaned up all the spills and left giggling after hearing James repeating like a broken record, "But madam, that's why the museum does not allow food and drink in the building."

Sam put away the mop and bucket, picked up a handful of cloths and a duster and headed to the dinosaur display after noticing it on the timetable workshop. She decided to walk past Mr Harman's office first and see if anyone was in there.

As she got closer, she noticed the door was open. A quick peek revealed it was empty, so she walked in.

It was as if nothing had ever happened. Not a single thing was out of place. Sam walked over to the desk and sat down in the leather chair, daring herself to open the drawer and look for the false bottom, but was startled by a loud female voice coming from the doorway. "Can I help you?"

"Oh, you scared me. Sorry, I was just dusting." Sam stood up immediately and moved away from the desk.

"What's your name? I haven't met you yet," the woman asked as she walked in and took the seat that Sam had vacated.

"I'm Samantha Page. Today is my first day back at work

after taking some time off," she replied, now calm and in control.

"So, you're Samantha. Nice to meet you. I'm Dr Julie Dunn. Please call me Julie. Can I call you Sam?" she asked while signalling her to sit down. Sam accepted with a nod.

"I'm acting director and CEO until a permanent replacement for Mr Harman is appointed. It was a terrible tragedy. We, everyone on the board, are all very sorry that you found him like that. It must have been awful. I hear you've undergone some counselling during your time off work. Have you found that helpful?"

"Yes, thanks. I am better now. I'll come back later to dust your office, Dr Dunn," Sam said, getting up from her chair.

"Please call me Julie, and my door is always open so pop in anytime. It was nice to meet you."

Sam could tell by the way she looked at her that Dr Dunn knew something was wrong. Hopefully, she would put it down to what she had experienced and wouldn't ask awkward questions. "Okay, nice to meet you too," she said politely as she walked out of the office.

Dr Dunn must be a board member and has been appointed as interim CEO. Sam was baffled about where that thought came from, especially after realising the book glasses were snuggled away in her pocket.

"Excuse me, young lady, I'm Professor Tenth and I'm late for my summer break lecture. My students and some colleagues are waiting for me in Lecture Room 1A, but my sense of direction is dreadful. Can you please help me? I would be most grateful," mumbled a gentle grey-haired older man in a grey suit.

"Follow me, professor, I would be happy to show you." Sam grinned and escorted him all the way.

"I needed a cup of coffee and they left me behind. Aren't

they all dreadful? I'm not so good with directions," the professor explained, trying not to spill his coffee while keeping up with her. "Thank you, you're very kind."

As they approached the huge double doors of the lecture theatre, the professor spilled his coffee all over his shoes and gasped at what he had done. Without any hesitation, Sam got on all fours and commenced cleaning the professor's shoes just as both doors swung open. The lecturer room erupted into laughter that echoed out and into the rest of the museum for all to hear.

Sam continued shining his shoes and finished cleaning the spill before standing up next to the professor. Her calmness and control surprised her. If something like this had happened before the book glasses had come into her possession, she would have felt humiliated in front of everyone and would have run off. However, she stood there facing him and accepted the professor's heartfelt thank you with a nod of her head while the crowd continued to roar in laughter.

As she turned to walk away, the man grabbed her arm and whispered in her ear. "I like your tenacity. You come with me, young lady."

Silence descended on the theatre as the students watched the professor lead her up to the lectern. Sam went with the flow.

"Good morning postgrads, I'd like to introduce you to... excuse me." He asked Sam her name. Then he continued with his arm still interlocked with hers.

"Human behaviour, ladies and gentlemen. What makes us different from our primeval ancestors? Physical action and observable emotion associated with individuals. We are in this magnificent building for a purpose. The University of Sydney has had a strong affiliation with the museum and that is why we have our summer seminar lectures here.

"You now have a chance to complete your thesis on human behaviour while the campus is closed during the Christmas break. Now, you are probably wondering why I asked Samantha to join me up here?"

A few of the students nodded their heads as he continued, "In my observations of human behaviour, most people when faced with a situation such as Samantha was faced with just now would have taken off like a scared animal. But even though she had a rather vocal audience, she ignored all of you and continued to clean the coffee off my shoes.

"My questions are—why did she react the way she did? And why wasn't she embarrassed? Welcome, all, to my lecture. And everyone, please give Samantha Page a huge round of applause to thank her for helping me with my introduction." The professor turned towards Sam and smiled.

The one hundred and fifty postgraduate students and the professor's colleagues all applauded. Impressed by his introduction, Sam gave him a nod of gratitude.

He retrieved a copy of a textbook and handed it over to her with his business card. "I authored this book. Consider it a gift. I hope you enjoy it. And if you ever consider tertiary education, be sure and contact me."

She accepted them with thanks and walked out of the theatre to another round of applause, feeling ten feet tall.

Things were changing for Sam and she knew it.

A SISTER'S HEARTBREAK

Closing the theatre doors behind her, Sam was energised with a new sense of excitement that the professor's gift had given her. The idea of studying at this level had never occurred to her before, but with the book glasses in her possession, this path was open to her.

Later, she joined Tom for lunch at the museum's café. He remained silent as she told him of her desire to study at university. After they had both finished their lunch, he told her to go home. His sympathetic look made Sam feel that he was confusing her sudden desire for university with the ongoing reaction to the trauma she'd experienced over Mr Harman's murder.

Sam didn't argue and, upon arriving in her apartment, immediately started to read the textbook the professor had given her. Although the book was not her cup of tea, she quickly finished it and still loved the idea of university. After changing out of her work clothes, she'd decided to go and visit Sue at the refuge when she heard a knock at her front door.

"Are you alright, sweetheart? It's Sister Sue!"

"Hi, Sister, yes I'm fine, thank you. Please come in."

"Where have you been? We've all missed you. The girls are asking me daily about you. We've all been worried sick." Sister Sue took the single seat at the kitchen table.

"I have so much to tell you. I was just getting ready to come and see you," Sam said as she retrieved some orange juice from the refrigerator.

"You wouldn't lie to a sister, and an old one at that, would you?" she said.

"It's true, no joke," Sam said as she filled two glasses with orange juice and then set out an assortment of pastries on a plate.

"Hang on a minute, what is going on, young lady? Orange juice and pastries? Let me look at this fridge." She walked over to open it. "You have food in here, Sam. How on earth did you fit all of that in this tiny little thing?"

"That's why I was coming to see you. I wanted to tell you that I have my own money and I don't need to take any more food or anything else from the refuge." Sam then opened the pantry door to show Sue that it was also well-stocked.

"So, you finally listened to me. That's terrific, Sam." Sue sat back down, her eyes shining.

The two women spent the afternoon eating, drinking, and enjoying each other's company with Sister Sue sitting on the only chair while Sam sat on an old footstool. Sam loved her company as Sue was like a mother to her.

Then she saw Sue's eyes fall on the professor's textbook and switch to the other books she'd borrowed from the library. A frown appeared on her face and Sam remembered that the sister knew that she couldn't read.

"What are all these books doing here?" she said.

"They are my books," Sam mumbled through a mouthful of food.

"Really? But you told me you can't read because of your dyslexia."

"I know, but now I can. I was going to tell you. It's great, isn't it? Aren't you happy for me?" She hoped the sister wouldn't ask too many difficult questions.

Fortunately, she directed the conversation back to her work at the museum. Then she told Sam she needed to get back to the refuge and get ready for dinner. They both stood and Sam opened the door.

"So, I guess we won't see you much at the refuge. The girls are going to miss you," Sue said on her way out the door.

"Not much, but I will drop in from time to time. I won't forget you, Sister Sue." Sam winked before filling her mouth with another pastry.

———

Sue closed the door behind her before bursting into tears. Over the last five years, she had known this was going to happen one day. In the early years, she'd dared it to happen, even wished for it with all her heart. Now she cursed the day she had longed for it.

Her faith in God had given her the strength to continue life's journey and she believed her prayers had been answered five years before, when Sam had come into her life. It had been a joyous day. Sam had been helpless, vulnerable and in need of care.

The first time she'd seen Sam walk into her office at the refuge to enquire about volunteering, Sue had immediately felt a connection with her. As a rule, eighteen-year-old girls who looked the way she did, did not spend much time volunteering.

Once she'd realised who Sam was, she hadn't been able to believe it. Sam, of all people, had come to her! Sam had given her a new direction, washing away her despair. She had replaced the emptiness with purpose.

Sue pondered what Sam had said about being able to read. It didn't make sense that one minute she couldn't read and the next she could. But then, she had kept her secret from the girl, one that could have altered the course of her life, so it wasn't like she could judge. What was she going to do without Sam's regular visits to the refuge? It was devastating to imagine life without her.

All the way back to the refuge Sue dragged her feet, trying to think of other ways she could continue to see Sam because she couldn't accept a life without her.

"Mummy, Mummy, wake up!"

It was Sam's voice, but Sue couldn't open her eyes. What had happened?

That's right. She'd found Joyce on the floor next to her bed, the half-empty bottle of sleeping pills beside her. It had been an impulsive decision, borne out of grief, to snatch up the bottle and swallow the rest. Consumed with grief at the loss of her husband, like Joyce was, she hadn't thought of her daughter.

She heard her in-laws' voices, then someone she didn't know. Then there was nothing until she woke up.

Mary, her mother-in-law, was sitting beside her. "I'm so glad to see your eyes open."

But it hurt to open them. "Where am I?"

"The hospital. Joyce is here too. They got to you in time to save both of you. But why did you do it?"

She sighed. "I couldn't stand it anymore. The house is too empty." Waking up a little more, she looked around the room. "Samantha! Where is she?"

Mary put out a hand to calm her. "Hush. She's staying with us."

But that only brought more guilt. Why hadn't she thought

about what this would mean for her daughter? "How much longer am I going to be here?"

"I don't know. Maybe a couple of days."

"Can you bring Sam in to see me?"

But Mary's face was grave. "I'm sorry, but they don't think that's a good idea right now."

They didn't think it was a good idea for her to see her daughter? "Who?"

"The Department of Human Services. They think she should be in our care for now."

Sue sat straight up in bed, the room spinning. "For how long?"

She didn't trust her mother-in-law's smile. "Why don't you get better and then we'll see?"

NEGOTIATIONS

The next morning at work things started heating up between Tom and some of the contract staff who were disputing the hours they worked over the weekend. Sam walked in to find him arguing with two people representing the contract staff. They didn't give him a chance to get a word in and just kept on shouting at him.

"Back off, both of you, and take it up with management. You know very well that Tom can't help you with that issue. Go and see Dr Julie Dunn. If you don't leave now, I'll call security," Sam yelled.

When the workers realised she was right, they apologised and marched out of the workshop.

"Thanks, Sam. I tried to talk to them, but they wouldn't listen. You were great. Well done." Tom kept smiling as he got ready to start work.

Later that morning, Sam was summoned to Dr Dunn's office.

"Come in, young lady. Please sit down," Dr Dunn said with a serious look on her face.

"Thank you, Dr Dunn," said Sam with a smile.

"Please call me Julie. You are getting quite a reputation around here, young lady." She walked around her desk to sit next to Sam.

"Really? I hope it's good."

"Yes, it's great. You made quite an impression on Professor Tenth, and then there was the way you negotiated with the workers for Tom this morning. I am impressed and let me tell you, I don't impress easily. You are on my radar and I'm keeping a close watch on you now."

"Thank you." Sam kept calm and felt good.

"Tell me, is there anything I can do for you?" Julie asked.

"No thanks, I'm fine."

"There must be something. Please tell me and it's yours."

"Well, I'm interested in going to university, but I don't know what the entrance requirements are to get in." Sam couldn't believe she'd said that.

"Don't you worry about that. Professor Tenth and I go way back. The first semester of the new year doesn't start until March, so we have plenty of time. In the meantime, I will organise a meeting with him and I'm sure he will be happy to help you. After all, you did make him look good yesterday." She wrote a note in her diary.

"Wow, thanks, Julie. I appreciate it." Sam couldn't hold back her excitement.

"So, what do you want to study at university?" Julie asked, placing her pen down.

"Law," said Sam as she stood up from her chair.

"You're a girl after my own heart; I did law many years ago. Good for you."

"I need to get back to work. Thank you so much for everything, Julie," Sam said.

"Yes, yes. As soon as I hear from the professor, I will contact you."

As she hurried back to the workshop, Sam pinched herself to see if she was dreaming. To be acknowledged by Julie was one thing, but for her to arrange a meeting with the professor was out of this world.

Although the prospect was exciting, Sam had knots in her stomach thinking about university and how she was going to study as she had never done it before. She reached into the concealed top pocket in her blouse to reassure herself that the book glasses were still there. They were and her confidence flooded back.

SHOPPING FOR ONE

For the rest of the day, Sam struggled to concentrate on her work as her thoughts drifted to the meeting with the professor that Julie had promised to arrange.

She was glad to get home and head out to do her grocery shopping. Until recently, going to the supermarket had been an occasional treat and she purchased only bare necessities, but with a regular wage, she planned to shop regularly.

Since moving to Sydney from Melbourne five years before, the refuge's leftovers had sustained her. But she was no longer that scared girl. She was determined to do this on her own.

Over the years, the constant failures of not securing a job and her lack of money to purchase even the basics to survive had reinforced her belief that she was a failure. But now she found herself in a delightful world of colours, aromas, and sounds. A euphoric feeling of exhilaration washed over her. She grabbed a shopping trolley, determined to take her time, and savour the experience. Taking joy in being one of a crowd of shoppers, nothing could get her down; she even loved the fact her trolley had a wobbly front wheel.

By the time she got to the third aisle, her trolley was three-quarters full. The more she filled it, the wobblier it got, but she didn't mind.

"You must have a big family to feed," said a tall shopper with braces on her teeth and a toddler in the trolley seat.

"Yes, I'm hungry," Sam explained seriously.

The lady started laughing. As she walked off with her son, she yelled, "Another comedian. That's just as funny as those glasses you're wearing!"

Sam paid for her shopping and organised to have it delivered to her apartment. Then she ventured off to purchase a mobile phone, a tablet, and a laptop computer at the nearby high-end shopping mall.

She was amazed to discover a huge number of brands and that they all came in various shapes and sizes and colours. The book glasses became very effective once she started reading about the features of each one.

She selected the latest models of the most appropriate devices for her purposes and used her debit card to pay for them. It had been almost six weeks since she'd started work at the museum and she couldn't believe how much money had accumulated in her bank account.

She immediately entered as many phone numbers as she could into her mobile phone, starting with her volunteer colleagues and the sisters at the refuge. Work numbers were easy because they had given her a contact list but getting details from those she knew from the refuge was more challenging as they were all on different shifts. She needed to pay them a visit.

———

"Hi, Sue. You got a minute?" asked Sam, eager and happy to see her.

Sue's eyes brightened over the bunch of flowers in her arms. "I have several minutes for you, Sam. Give me a second to put these flowers down. They are from Mary from next door again. I told her she'll go broke if she continues to give me flowers every day. I really don't know how she keeps that flower shop open. I never see customers in there."

She put the flowers in a vase on her desk and sat down in her office chair. "Okay, now that's done. Tell me what I can do for you, darling."

"I just got a mobile phone and I'd like to add your number to my contact list, please," Sam said.

She stared at Sam's glasses. "Where did you get those glasses? I didn't know you had glasses, my love." She reached out for them.

Ignoring her outstretched hand, Sam took off the glasses and placed them in her pocket. "No, I don't need glasses, I found them at work and sometimes put them on for fun, that's all. Anyway, here's my new mobile. Do you like it?"

Sue quickly forgot about the glasses and told Sam about all the mishaps and funny things that had occurred at the refuge while she had been away and entered her mobile number into Sam's phone. Sam breathed a sigh of relief. The less she talked about the glasses, the better. She scolded herself for wearing them constantly. She would have to be more careful.

MONDAYS

Monday was Sam's favourite day of the week at the museum because it was Tom's day off and she was left to allocate work herself.

She loved to take her duster and go sightseeing, pretending to dust all the displays. Always looking around first to ensure no one was watching, she put on the book glasses and opened up a new world of adventure every time she read the displays.

After checking the coast was clear, she picked up a huge book on dinosaurs and palaeontology. Sitting down in front of the T-rex full-sized skeleton, she commenced reading.

Evolution Periods

The Devonian Period about 410 to 360 million years ago —The first land animals evolve.

The Carboniferous Period about 360 to 260 million years ago—The tetrapods radiate.

The Permian Period about 290 to 250 million years— Reptiles first dominate the land.

The Triassic Period about 250 to 210 million years ago—
The evolution of the archosaurs and early dinosaurs.
The Jurassic Period about 210 to 150 million years ago—
Dinosaurs dominate the land.
The Cretaceous Period about 150 to 65 million years ago
—The greatest diversity of dinosaurs.
The evolution periods are documented...

The glasses' lenses darkened, and Sam looked up to see what was casting the shadow. Frightened, she dropped the book and fell backwards.

The glasses slipped down her nose and the shadow disappeared. But when she repositioned them, she was left breathless at what she saw.

The T-rex skeleton now had skin, teeth, claws, eyes and appeared fully intact before her. But when she took off the glasses, it turned back into a skeleton.

Sam took off the glasses and put them away, then carefully returned the book to its place on the lectern. She quickly retraced her steps to the workshop to hide. Fighting panic, she wondered what to do next. She spent her entire lunch break there and only left after being called to deal with a couple of spills in the foyer.

After work, she raced home and barricaded herself in her apartment, not knowing what she was afraid of.

She decided to put the glasses back on to calm herself down. As usual, they put her back in control and she was able to think straight once more. She made a delicious Quiche Lorraine in no time, opened a cheap bottle of Chardonnay, and ate her dinner while reading all the junk mail and magazines she'd collected from her letterbox.

A knock on the door startled her and she chuckled,

assuming it was Sister Sue coming for a cup of tea. She hurriedly took off the glasses and put them away under her top and went to open the door.

Two men in dark blue suits stood outside. "Hello, are you Samantha Page?" one of the men asked in a deep voice. He was holding a folder full of papers.

"Yes, I'm Sam. Who are you?"

"I'm Detective Terry Roth and this is Detective Jason Gower. Can we come in, please?" He held out a badge and identification.

Sam showed them in and they each took a seat around the small worn-out kitchen table, Detective Roth pulling up the footstool. She desperately wanted to put on the book glasses but didn't dare.

"Ma'am, we are investigating the murder of Mr Charles Harman. Thank you for your statement back at the police station. We have just become aware of new information and are hoping you can help us with it." Detective Roth opened his folder and showed her some large black and white photos.

"What are they?" Sam asked, trying to conceal the fact she recognised the object in the pictures.

"Mr Harman had a false bottom on one of his desk drawers in which we believe he kept a pair of reading glasses, the same ones that appear in these photos. Can you tell us anything about these glasses?" He stared into her eyes.

For the first time in her life, Sam didn't panic and stared right back at him without blinking. "No, I'm sorry, I can't."

"You didn't mention them in your statement; here's a copy for you. We were hoping that maybe we could help you remember something by showing you these photos, that's all."

"No, nothing, sorry. I can't help you."

"Here, have a closer look." Detective Roth handed her the photos and both detectives looked at her curiously.

"Why am I looking at black and white photos of reading glasses? Are they Mr Harman's?" She put the photos back down on the table.

"The three men who allegedly murdered Mr Harman were apparently after these glasses because they are unique and extremely valuable. Our sources refer to them as 'The Holy Book Glasses' and they are believed to have been made in Europe, most likely Rome, over three hundred years ago. The glasses are priceless, and a seller could pretty much set any price for them. But what is of great concern to us is that there are some people of interest to us who want to get their hands on these glasses and would do anything to do so."

She gave nothing away and shook her head. "Why are they called Holy Book Glasses?"

"Apparently, they were made for the pope of the day and his successors," the detective said after checking his notebook.

"Why did Mr Harman have them?"

"We don't know but we believe the three men murdered him before taking them."

"So, they took the glasses," Sam said, almost smiling. "And that's why they murdered him."

"That's right. Look, we are not leaving any stone unturned. If you can help us with anything, please call us. If you remember something, whether tomorrow or next week, please don't hesitate to contact us. We would appreciate your cooperation."

"Sure, if I remember anything, I will." She looked away to try to conceal her relief that they didn't suspect her.

"Thank you for your time. Here's my card," said Detective Roth before placing the photos back in his folder.

Sam silently walked the detectives to the door and let them out. She watched them walk away, closed and locked the door, then leant heavily against it.

They didn't suspect she had anything to do with the missing glasses. She put them back on to read the copy of her police statement they had left behind.

Although the glasses in the photos resembled hers, fortunately, they showed mostly the case and not a close-up of the glasses themselves. She was delighted that they didn't reveal all the fine details of the Latin script etched into the metal frames.

Once composed and confident again, she was determined not to waste another moment thinking about what could or may happen; she had the glasses and was going to make the most of them. She felt it might be a good idea to have a similar pair made in case someone who had noticed her using them told the police about it. The only thing she knew for sure was that she couldn't lose them, not now.

———

The next day at work, Sam noticed the same two detectives in Julie's office. They stayed there most of the morning, so she kept well away, fearing another interrogation. Once they had gone, she moved on to more important things like planning which books to read next.

Sam discovered that the glasses weren't effective when reading from a computer or her mobile phone; the visions and transfer of knowledge did not work. So, it was back to the library after work to borrow some books to take home.

She deliberated over what to read next. She was done with cooking and grocery shopping tips and ideas. Learning other languages was now appealing to her. Fashions and cosmetics were also of interest as she wanted to work on her appearance and develop a new style. Or perhaps mathematics and economics would be a good place to start.

Learning was her only focus now and gave her a high she had never experienced before. *Who knew?* she thought. It was incredible to think that something which such a short time ago had been impossibly difficult for her was now so easy.

MANLY FERRY

The next day after work, Sam couldn't wait to get to the library. On her way home, she dropped in and chose a selection of books. Once dinner was out of the way, she climbed into bed, put on the glasses, and looked at them.

She had selected *Mathletics* by Wayne L Winston, *Advanced Math* by Richard G. Brow, and *Fundamentals of Economics* by Dr William Boyes. So, she started reading them.

On the following Saturday, she had the urge to visit Sue and tell her all about her plan to take the ferry to Manly. Her excitement was unmatched and her confidence high now she had a little money to finally indulge herself. But first, she would take her time getting ready.

After her shower, with a towel wrapped around her, she put on the glasses, eagerly opened her new makeup kit, and gleefully read out the names of each item: 'Concealer, foundation, blush, translucent powder, mascara, neutral eye shadow, defining eye shadow and eyeliner.'

Then, standing in her dingy old bathroom with its peeling paint and stained and cracked tiles, she started to rapidly read

Do Your Makeup Like the Stars, a how-to pull-out brochure from a women's magazine. In no time, she had read it and tossed it to one side.

Sam was suddenly an expert in applying her makeup, instinctively choosing the right colours and tones to match her fair skin, blue eyes, and brown hair. Keeping the glasses on, although she had to hold them in front of her face to do her eyes and cheeks, the more she took her time, the faster she got. The result was a sophisticated look that only someone practised could achieve.

She put on the dress she had received from Sue one Christmas a few years before. Her black strapless bra fitted well under the black strapless tube top dress, but her usual basic cotton bikini briefs were out of the question under the form-fitting dress. Instead, she selected a new black lace G-string.

Pleased with the look, she hurriedly strapped on her black summer sandals, grabbed her imitation black leather back and shoulder bag and left the apartment. Her glasses were safely nestled in her bag that she wore backwards to keep a close eye on it.

"Who is this thing of beauty? It can't be Sam! Is that really you?" Sue's voice echoed through the main hall and into the kitchen, drawing everyone out to see for themselves.

"Look what you've done. Everyone heard you," Sam said with a smile as she dangled her handbag, back and forth, from one hand.

The entire staff and the few volunteers rushed out to see what the fuss was about.

"Is that our Samantha in that little black number?" one of the volunteers said.

"You finally decided to wear it," Sister Sue said proudly.

"You look different, Sam. I mean, aside from the dress, you're another person. Who did your hair and make-up?" Jan asked.

"I did it all myself. You like it?" Sam half-smiled and struck a fashion shoot pose.

They all stood there open-mouthed, until a long-term homeless woman, Betty, walked in and screamed, "You think you're better than us, do you? Piss off! You think you're a posh bitch."

"Betty, that's our Sam. Don't you upset her when she's gone to all that trouble. You apologise right now. Sorry, Sam. Betty must be back on the drink," Jan said.

"Sorry, Sam. I didn't fucking recognise you," Betty said, prompting everyone to erupt into laughter, including Samantha.

"Okay ladies, enough of that. Back to work, please. Betty, you come with me, love. Sam, let me deal with her and then come and see me in my office," Sue said.

"Maybe later, Sue. I'm going to Manly for the day, so see ya," she said with a nod and walked out, still swinging her bag. She saw the disappointed look on Sue's face and promised herself that she would come back soon to fill her in on the day.

———

After boarding the Manly ferry, Sam took a seat on the top deck and savoured the moment with a selfie. She remembered to remove the glasses, having vowed to never to take a photo with them on. The thought of losing them was too frightening to contemplate.

She felt a jolt on her left arm as someone sat down next to her and bumped her. Annoyed, she glanced over and was pleasantly surprised to find it was a youngish man with golden hair who was reading text messages on his phone.

Trying her best not to show any interest, she gazed out her window, looking at the reflections in the glass to see if she could locate any vacant seats and figure out why he'd picked the seat next to her.

The man accidentally dropped his phone and it landed on her foot.

"Here you go," Sam said as she handed it to him.

"Wow, thanks, gorgeous. It just slipped. Sorry about that. I'm Billy. Well, my name is William Ashley, but everyone calls me Billy. What's your name?" He smiled.

"Samantha, hi," she replied, taking a good look at him. Handsome, with hazel eyes, short blond hair and a solid physique, he was probably about thirty years old. He was wearing a yellow smiley-face T-shirt, blue jeans, and runners, but she noticed he wore no wedding ring.

"Hi, Samantha. Where are you going?"

"Manly."

"Yeah, me too. Are you visiting someone? A boyfriend, maybe?"

"No boyfriend. Just sightseeing, that's all."

"So, you're not visiting your boyfriend, or you don't have a boyfriend?" he asked.

Sam didn't know what to say and Billy's grin grew even larger as he waited for a reply. Finally, she said, "No to both. Where are you going?"

"I'm going home. I live in Manly. And before you ask, no girlfriend! I just split up with her. Actually, she split up with me. She found someone at uni and dumped me. Apparently, I'm not as smart as he is because I didn't go to uni," Billy said, still wearing the same large grin.

"Sorry to hear that," Sam said sincerely.

"That's okay. It wasn't going anywhere. For the last couple of weeks, she'd been avoiding me and because of my work, I only had the weekends free to see her. I finally tracked her down at her uni apartment today and that's when she told me. With no texts or calls for a couple of weeks, I knew this was going to happen. It didn't take a genius to figure out she had someone else. Her loss."

"What do you do for work?" Sam asked.

"I work in construction on building sites. I mainly do hard labouring work, but I enjoy it and it keeps me fit. What do you do?"

"I work at the Australian Museum as a laboratory technician. That's a fancy way to say cleaner." Sam felt great saying that for the first time to a stranger.

"That's great. I was afraid you were going to say you're a uni student." Billy's large grin swiftly reappeared.

"No, I wish." Sam smiled back.

They were deep in conversation when the ferry docked and she followed him down the gangway, hardly aware they had arrived at Manly Wharf. Sam had been so focused on her chat with Billy, she had forgotten to enjoy her much-anticipated ferry ride.

"Where are you off to now, Samantha? What sights would you like me to show you?" Billy asked.

"No, don't be silly. I'm sure you have better things to do," Sam said, hoping he didn't.

"No, I have all weekend free. Remember, I have no girl-friend now. Also, Manly is my home and I would love to show you around. How about it?"

"Okay, great. Where do we go first?" Sam's heart beat fast with excitement. Exploring Manly was no longer her main priority as Billy had fully captured her attention, filling her imagination with unbelievable hopes, desires, and dreams.

As they walked past a shop window, she caught a glimpse of their reflection in the glass. She was exhilarated to notice he stood so much taller than her and was impressed with his brawny appearance. His voice was calming and his attention to detail in describing things was impressive. But in-between describing all that Manly had to offer, she loved that not only did he let her talk, but he also seemed interested in what she had to say.

Billy insisted on shouting her a traditional fish and chips lunch, which they ate sitting at the beach on the sand barricade wall as the locals did. This was followed by a lengthy walk to Shelly Beach via the breathtaking, attention-grabbing, and romantic Marine Parade walkway. At one stage, nearly halfway down the walkway, she got goosebumps when she felt his hand slightly touch hers as they walked.

The late afternoon sun was still warm when a refreshing sea breeze started to blow. Billy was still playing tour guide. The day had been something out of a fairy tale for Sam. She would never have believed something like this could ever happen to her.

Where did he come from? she wondered as they walked along talking about silly things like the weather, ferry times and seasonal crowds on the beach. *How did this happen to me?*

The minutes had turned into hours when Sam was shocked to notice the sun was casting shadows of the beachfront buildings over Manly Beach. "I need to go now," she said, wishing the magical day could continue.

"Do you need to be anywhere?" Billy asked. "If you don't, how about we go to the Star Casino for dinner?"

"Where?"

"Wow, you haven't been there, awesome. We've got to go now."

"Is it far?"

"It's on your side, so we need to catch a ferry back but instead of getting off at Circular Quay, we get off at the wharf at Darling Harbour."

"I know where that is," said Sam. "Okay."

"One small problem—I can't take you to dinner looking like this." He looked down at his T-shirt and jeans. "Can you come with me to my place so I can get changed? It's only a few streets from here. Is that okay?"

"Yeah, sure." Sam nodded.

"I live in a one-bedroom apartment. You probably live in a house?" Billy's grin left him.

"No."

"It's a one-bedroom apartment with a separate kitchen, bathroom and lounge but I love its beachside view. It is small, but new and that's all I can afford." He looked a little embarrassed.

"Don't worry, my apartment is not much different. I have a small bedroom with a tiny bathroom that hasn't been renovated since who knows when."

"That's great. I mean, it's not great but at least you understand how expensive apartments are. It's small but on a positive note, it's new and I like the views. I'm renting, but one day I would like to buy it when I get the money for the deposit. The ex-girlfriend was not impressed at all when I showed her where I lived. I'm glad you're not like that, Sam."

He let them into his apartment, quickly changed and then proudly showed off his Australian coin collection. Sam was impressed with the great lengths he had gone to acquire the coins, lining up for hours or sometimes even days at Australia Post to purchase collector's editions of new coin releases.

Apart from being much newer, Billy's building and apartment were almost identical to her own and she was impressed with how clean and tidy he kept it.

On the return ferry ride, Sam let Billy do most of the talking because she was awestruck at the thought that she was going out to dinner with this gorgeous man. She had always imagined her ideal man as having dark hair and brown eyes, but she now thought that blonde hair and hazel eyes were pretty close to perfect. She discovered he was twenty-five years old and an only child, raised by his mother after his father left them both just after he was born.

Before she knew it, they were disembarking at Darling Harbour. After a brisk walk to Star Casino, they entered the foyer and were immersed in a magnificent atmosphere full of lights, glamour, and movement. Sam had been unaware the place existed so close to both the refuge and her apartment.

As they walked among the crowd, Billy took the opportunity to hold her hand, explaining that he didn't want to lose her. They made their way through the thick crowd, wearing matching grins.

The wing section of the casino was devoted to restaurants and was a sight to behold. Sam was amazed at the variety of offerings from high-end exclusive restaurants right through to eateries displaying ten-dollar steak and chips specials. A little overwhelmed with the selection, she was relieved when Billy shouted over the noise. "Do you like Chinese food?"

"Yes, I love fried rice," she yelled back.

"Great. Chinese it is." Billy led the way, still holding her hand.

They both ordered fried rice and shared a main meal of sweet and sour pork and Sam ordered a glass of Chardonnay while Billy requested a beer.

After dinner, they agreed to try their luck in the casino. Sam didn't care where they went as long as Billy kept on holding her hand.

Passing through an even denser crowd, Sam ensured her

bag was securely strapped to her chest and clutched Billy's arm with both hands, loving every minute of the extra contact.

They watched the roulette wheel, and she was fascinated by the ball bouncing around and landing mostly on black numbers.

"What do you think, Samantha?" Billy asked.

"Wow, glitzy, fun, bright and fantastic," she said.

She couldn't believe the noise in the casino. It was deafening, especially from the slot machines. Two main sounds echoed repeatedly and continuously. First, there was the sound of a "three-ping defeat", followed by some swearing and muttering and eventually another coin flowing through the slot. The second was three pings, a hush and then the jittering fall of coins, followed by a lot more swearing. In the latter case, the swearing was more joyous and energetic.

Without Billy noticing, Sam whipped on the book glasses to take a closer look at the roulette game to work out, for herself, the expected value of a black number winning or a red number winning. She quickly calculated that red had the probability of winning eighteen red numbers from a total of thirty-eight black and red numbers, which equalled 0.473 or 47.3%. It was a little less than 50% for a win.

She effortlessly worked out the expected value (EV), which was the weighted average of how much she could win or lose. Therefore, EV–1 (18/38) for red + (-1) (20/38) for black = -2/38 = -0.0526, which meant, on average, she would lose -5.26 cents for every dollar spent at the roulette table whether she put her money on the black or red numbers.

Next, she focused on the odds for the first-to-twelve odds section of the roulette table and calculated that every dollar on the first-to-twelve section would pay her modest two to one odds. The probability of a two-dollar win was 12/38 and the probability of a one-dollar loss was 26/38. The expected value

(1st 12) = 2 (12/38) = (-1) (26/38) = -2/38 = -0.0526 = -5.3 cents, which was a disadvantage on average.

Turning her focus to any single number on the roulette table, she worked out that the chance of an individual number winning was thirty-five to one. As the probability of a thirty-five win was 1/38, and the probability of a loss worked was 37/38, the expected value was EV = 35 (1/38) = (-1) (37/38 = -2/38 = -0.0526 = -5.3 cents.

Overall, she concluded that every bet would have the same negative value of -5.3 cents per one dollar bet on average across the entire game.

Having a better idea of how it all worked, Sam took off the glasses before Billy noticed.

"I love blackjack, Sam. Do you know what blackjack is?"

Loving how Billy whispered intimately in her ear, she whispered back, "No."

"I'm not very good but I enjoy it. Do you want to come and watch me play?"

"Sure."

They found a blackjack table with a spare seat and Billy said, "Look after this seat for me. I'll be back soon."

When he returned with a heap of colourful plastic disks with numbers on them, she asked, "What are they?"

"They're casino chips. You can't play with real money, so you need to buy casino chips and use them to bet instead. See how the others around the table are doing it?"

"Okay." She pulled out the chair to take a seat.

"No, you can't sit down, they'll think you're a player," said Billy.

Sam backed away and Billy sat down and put his pile of chips on the table in front of him. "Sorry, I'll just stand here behind you."

Five drinks later, Billy was down to less than half of his five-hundred-dollar pile of chips. Sam guessed that he was embarrassed that she was watching him lose but he grinned every time he turned to look at her.

Annoyed that his competitors were getting the upper hand, Sam took out the book glasses to try them out.

As usual, everything became brighter and more enhanced. She was astonished to discover the ability to identify every card, no matter what position the dealer placed them on the table. By this stage, a crowd had started to build, and onlookers were being pushed back by security staff to keep everyone a safe distance from the players.

With the glasses on, she quickly gleaned an understanding of the game and realised Billy was coming close to losing all his chips. *The game is easy,* she thought, *let the dealer draw additional cards until the hand exceeds a total amount of twenty-one.*

She was confident she could do better than Billy. But how would she get him to let her take his place at the table?

Out of the blue, Billy said, "Samantha, can you take my place while I'll go the toilet, please?"

"Yes, I would love too."

"Sorry, but I only have one hundred dollars in chips left for you. Are you okay to play a hand or two while I'm away?"

"Sure, I'll be fine," she said, and he raced off in a hurry.

After greeting everyone around the table with a nod of her head, she started by placing a twenty-dollar chip on the first card, the five of spades. After going around the table without anyone going bust, that is, the total value of their cards not exceeding twenty-one, all eyes were on Sam and the dealer dealt her next card, which was the six of hearts.

Matching the bets of the others, she increased her bet by another forty dollars and then put the rest of Billy's chips on the pile before calling out for the dealer to "hit" her with another card. She felt great saying that after hearing all the players saying it for the last hour.

The dealer produced the two of clubs and she immediately asked for another hit that ended up being the three of diamonds, making her fours cards now total sixteen.

Caught up in the anticipation of the game, the crowd went so quiet you could hear a pin drop. Billy returned from the bathroom and she could see he was shocked that she had all his chips on one bet.

The dealer asked her, "Would you like to stand or have another hit?"

After tapping her shoulder to get her attention, Billy shook his head and silently but mouthed, "NO."

She turned back to the dealer and asked for another hit. Her fifth card was a five of diamonds, totalling twenty-one. She turned back to see the joy in Billy's face as he called out, "Blackjack!"

The other players and the crowd waited expectantly as the dealer faced each of the other players in turn and gave them the same choice, to stand or have another hit. All declined another card, except for the last player, sitting on Sam's right, who wore a black pinstripe suit and sunglasses. He said, "Hit me." When the king of spades hit the table, he grimaced and then nodded at Sam, admitting defeat.

Billy let out a whoop. "You just won one hundred dollars on top of the original one hundred I left you with. How did you do that?"

"It's a numbers game, plus lady luck has a lot to do with it," said the player in the pinstripe suit.

"Yes, a numbers game," said Sam with a smile.

"Come on, let's take our winnings and get out of here. What do you say?" Billy kissed her on the cheek.

Surprised, Sam nodded. Her heart started beating quickly

as she followed him to the bar. Billy ordered a beer and a Chardonnay, then they found a booth and sat opposite each other.

As he talked about her win, she gazed into his eyes. Her desire for him was building and she didn't know how to control it. The book glasses couldn't help her this time and it was driving her crazy. The more he talked, the more she desired him.

"What's wrong?" Billy asked.

"I managed to double the one hundred dollars you left me and all you give me is a peck on the cheek?" Sam said.

"Say no more, gorgeous, get ready for the best kiss of your life," Billy whispered. He got out of his seat and went around and took her into his arms. Then he delivered on his promise, right there in the crowded bar.

They cuddled up in the booth and kissed, and neither of them was going to stop anytime soon. Sam had been waiting forever for someone to enter her life and she wasn't going to let go now. She held on to Billy as if her life depended on him.

"Let's rent a room here, at the casino tonight. What do you think?" Billy asked before again kissing her.

Sam's heart raced at his suggestion. But she knew that if this was going to last, she needed to control herself, at least for the moment. She slowly shook her head.

"Sorry, I couldn't help myself. I shouldn't have asked." Billy kissed the corner of her mouth and left a trail of wet kisses along her jaw and down her neck.

Sam pulled back. "I need to go home now," she said but immediately regretted her words.

"I'll walk you home. Please let me walk you home. I promise I won't come in."

"I would love that, thank you," she said and gave him a crushing hug.

Billy's eyes lit up like fireflies. He was up in a flash, holding out his hand to her as she clambered out of the booth.

They made their way out of the casino and onto the street. The city lights looked brighter than usual and Sam was shocked to discover it was now five past eleven. "Where did the time go?" she asked.

"I don't know. It happens to me every time I go into the casino. Is it okay if I hold your hand?"

"I would like that very much," Sam replied with a large grin.

Holding hands soon progressed to arms wrapped around each other's waists, nice and secure, but not too tight. Their conversation dropped off as Sam focused more on the feel of Billy's arms around her, and their leisurely walk slowed to a snail's pace.

"We're here," she said abruptly.

"Already?" Billy looked disappointed.

"Do you want to come in?"

"Of course, but no thanks. I wouldn't be able to control myself so I'd better not. Maybe next time."

"Okay, see ya." Sam started walking to the front door of her building, aching for one last kiss.

"Wait a minute, wait a minute, you must give me your mobile number... and a kiss goodnight," Billy said with a grin.

"What do you want first?" Sam teased.

She got her goodnight kiss and Billy got her number and stole a second quick kiss. They parted ways, both smiling widely, and Sam couldn't wait until their rendezvous the following Saturday at noon on Manly Wharf.

After several text messages back and forth to Billy, she went to bed on cloud nine and fell asleep as soon as her head hit the pillow. One of her dreams had finally become a reality and she was beside herself with happiness.

MAKING SOME MONEY

The following morning after breakfast, Sam decided to skip Sunday morning prayers with Sister Sue at the refuge and head back to the casino. She hoped God would understand, even if Sister Sue did not. If she could make some money, she could give up her job at the museum and go to university.

The idea of winning enough money to allow her to give up her job was appealing, but the challenge was how much she could win without drawing unwanted attention to herself.

Pondering that idea, she had a shower, got dressed and strolled towards the casino. She dressed inconspicuously in long dark blue trousers with a short-sleeved white lace top and low-heeled black sandals with ankle and foot straps.

As she walked, she tried to put Billy out of her mind and focus on the challenges ahead.

It was a bright clear sunny day and she stopped and took a seat on one of many benches alongside the water. She calmly took out the book glasses and put them on and headed into the casino. Bypassing the slot machines and the roulette table, she headed straight to the blackjack table after changing one hundred dollars into casino chips.

The atmosphere was no different from the night before. The table was almost empty, apart from two people on the other side who looked like they had been there all night and were almost out of chips.

As she placed her chips down, she was amazed to notice the superb light show was just as effective as it had been the night before. She immediately noticed the dealer's card dispenser was full with a fresh set of no fewer than eight decks of cards.

From that moment, it was game on for Sam and, in less than an hour, she turned her one hundred dollars into two thousand. An hour later, after noticing a crowd building, she decided to take a break. She picked up her chips and took them to the cashier window to cash them in.

"Congratulations. Can I have some ID please?" the cashier said. "And I'll print out your cheque."

"Excuse me, but why are you giving me a cheque when I gave you cash?" Sam asked.

"It's casino policy, ma'am."

Sam produced her ID and took the cheque for five thousand, two hundred and fifty dollars and placed it in her purse. Her stomach growled so she set off to find somewhere to have lunch.

Taking her time at a salad bar, she kept the glasses on and looked around to see if anyone was following her. This was the first time she had worn the glasses for any length of time, and she had started to notice a transparent ball of lights appearing and disappearing around her. Assuming it was reflections from the extravagant casino lighting, she ignored it.

As she headed back into the casino, Sam decided to give poker a whirl and converted her cheque back into chips at the same cashier window. She found a game in play and, after observing a few rounds, took a seat at the table. When a new game started, she swiftly placed a five-hundred-dollar pile of chips down to scare the other players right from the start.

After the first round, all the players folded except a man with a beard who sat opposite Sam. He was persistent, losing almost fifteen hundred dollars in one game, but once the stakes increased to two thousand dollars, he folded and left the table.

Sam took the opportunity to continue with even stronger bets, but the other players become more unsure about playing after watching the bearded man leave. It had been nearly two hours since she'd returned from lunch.

"Excuse me, ma'am, casino management would like to talk to you when you're ready," a well-groomed man in a casino uniform whispered in her ear after she'd won another game.

Curious, Sam said, "I'm ready now."

"This way, please. Just leave your chips and we will have someone collect them for you."

Sam was led into a plush stateroom lounge where she was given drinks and food and offered the choice of an array of gifts from pens and key rings, through to more expensive items like watches, jewellery, earrings, bags, and bracelets.

"Hello, Samantha. I'm Frederick Hans, casino manager." Looking impressive in an immaculate black suit, he welcomed her with a sincere smile.

"Hello, Frederick. You have a natural Aussie accent but with a German name, I think?" Sam asked, trying to make small talk.

"Yes, I was born in Germany and my family came to Australia when I was five. It looks like you are enjoying your day here with us. On behalf of the casino, I would like to congratulate you on your winnings, and I would like to invite you to our VIP Premium Gaming Room. Your chips are waiting there for you."

Frederick's invitation was both surprising and appealing. "You mean the high roller room," Sam replied, recalling Billy telling her about it. "That's very kind of you, thank you." She sipped her complimentary Chardonnay and took another delicious hors d'oeuvre.

"It's my pleasure, Samantha. May I say your glasses are very unusual, they look very old. May I have a closer look, please?" He walked up next to her and reached out and almost touched them.

"Yes, they're my grandmother's. I got new lenses put in them and wear them to have something to remember her by. Please don't touch them." Sam took a step back out of his reach.

After politely withdrawing his hand, Fredrick explained there were various levels of VIP Premium Gaming Rooms. "With your winnings now a little over ten thousand dollars, you are certainly eligible for our entry-level room."

Sam felt like a special customer as she followed Shaun, an executive-level staff member assigned to cater to her every need, into an entry-level VIP room. Apart from the smaller crowd, who were all lavishly dressed, it didn't look any different.

When she took a seat at the main poker table, the weird visions of translucent lights started appearing again but this time they were in the shapes of people and one was walking towards her. Terrified, Sam ripped off the glasses and got up and asked Shaun to direct her to the toilets. Once inside the opulent bathroom, she splashed water over her face to refresh herself and looked around, thankful that the visions had gone.

After quickly relieving herself and washing her hands, she put the glasses back on. Once again, she was subject to the frightening ghost-like visions. However, this time there were more of them. The figures looked like lifeless people who were gone from this earth and roaming around aimlessly.

Then it came to her—perhaps this was a side effect of wearing the book glasses for too long. This was certainly the longest she had worn them. But why ghost-like visions and would they appear again? Going back out to play was impossible so she would need to exit without too much fuss.

With the book glasses in her hand, she walked out of the bathroom and asked Shaun to help her leave, explaining that she had left her medication at home and needed to leave immediately. Shaun had her cashed up and out of the casino in no time without asking any questions.

After racing home, Sam stowed the book glasses in their case and hid it in her closet. She then retrieved the casino's cheque from her purse and was pleased to discover the amount was a total of $10,755. For her, it was like having a million dollars, and she jumped up and down, screaming with joy. She was confident she could survive a long time before going back to work.

Sam also remembered reading, in one of her Australian tax law books, that her winnings would not be subject to government tax so she would be able to keep the lot. However, she did recall any interest from her winnings was subject to government tax, unfortunately.

In the morning she would call to inform Tom that she would no longer be able to work at the museum because returning each day to the scene of Mr Harman's murder was too traumatic for her.

UNDERGRADUATE

"Hello, Sam. It's Dr Julie Dunn from the museum," said the caller when Sam answered her mobile just after nine on Monday morning.

"Oh, hello, Dr Dunn, can I help you?"

"Tom just told me you called him to say you will not be back to work because you are still having issues dealing with Charles Harman's murder. My dear, you take all the time you need. I have arranged counsellors again for you so don't worry about a thing. We are all here for you, my dear. You have my mobile number now so if you feel like talking or when you are ready to come back, please feel free to call me any time, okay?"

"Thank you, Dr Dunn, it means a great deal to me that you called."

"I know this is a bad time, but Professor Kenneth Tenth just called me and would like to meet you if you're still interested in furthering your studies. If not, I'll text you his mobile number and you can call him when you feel like it."

"Wow, that's very nice of him. Yes, please," Sam said calmly, trying not to show too much excitement.

"Okay, bye for now." Dr Dunn hung up without waiting for her goodbye.

As soon as she received the professor's number, she called him and didn't even need to use the book glasses. "Hello, Professor. This is Samantha Page. Dr Dunn gave me your number."

"Yes, yes. You know I look after the Master of Clinical Psychology classes and also supervise several research PhD students here at the University of Sydney. They are postgraduates, but if you are interested, I would be happy to introduce you to my colleagues who look after the undergraduate classes. What do you think, are you up for it?"

"Yes, Professor. I am interested in studying law."

"If you are thinking of perhaps a Bachelor of Arts degree, psychology could be your second major. How about that?" The professor sounded hopeful.

"Sounds good, but I really want to do law, sir," Sam said confidently, determined to not be coerced into going down a different path.

"Can't blame me for trying. Okay, today is Monday. How about we meet in my office on Thursday around 10:30 a.m.?" he said, now sounding slightly disinterested.

"Thank you very much. I look forward it," she said, full of gratitude.

Sam was overflowing with happiness and hopefulness at the thought of being able to study at university and how it could change her life. She shivered when she recalled the ghostly visions while wearing the book glasses. Her chances of succeeding at university were dependent upon the glasses, but the onset of these visions raised questions about her ability to continue to wear them.

She slumped down onto a chair at her kitchen table and wondered why the visions had suddenly appeared after all this time. It may have been a result of wearing the glasses for an extended period, but she still couldn't understand the ghost-like visions of people.

Her mobile buzzed with a text, interrupting her musings, but she couldn't read the name of the sender. Afraid of wearing the glasses again, she pushed her phone aside. A few minutes later it buzzed again, and she retrieved the book glasses. She'd had enough of thinking the worst and decided to take a gamble and put them back on. After all, it had been over twelve hours since she'd last worn them. Hopefully, that was an adequate break to avoid the visions re-appearing.

She put on the glasses. No visions! She let out the breath she hadn't realised she'd been holding.

The text message was from Billy. Sam's joy returned when she read his message. He said he couldn't wait until Saturday to see her and pleaded with her to meet him that day after work for a drink. She replied that the wait would be worth it and to leave it for Saturday as planned. His eagerness to see her again warmed her heart; absence did make the heart grow fonder, but she needed to focus on her upcoming meeting with the professor. Billy reluctantly agreed to wait and promised to minimise his texting until Saturday.

———

On Thursday, as she walked to the University of Sydney, Sam felt confident about meeting with the professor. Reading a strategic selection of academic law books aimed at undergraduate students over the past few days had prepared her for any entrance exam or pre-entry test to which she might be subjected.

Her self-confidence was at an all-time high. Also, via trial and error, she had discovered that the book glasses had a time limit of five hours. Wearing them any longer would result in the reappearance of the ghost-like visions.

She had been immensely relieved to work this out. Whether or not she took small or long breaks in-between, she couldn't wear them any longer than a maximum of five hours. After that, she had to take a minimum of twelve hours' break before attempting to wear them again. Anything less would result in the return of the horrible visions. Working this out over the last few days had been terrifying but gratifying.

"This time it is you who is lost, and it is I who can assist in showing you the way. Welcome, Samantha, welcome indeed," said the professor, coming up from behind her.

"Hello, Professor. How did you know I was here?" Sam asked with a smile.

"Simple. I'm old and wise, you see. Not really. I saw you coming in from my office window." He seemed delighted in her laugh. "That's a most impressive suit you have on, very lovely indeed. You certainly look much different from the way you did when we first met. Good for you."

He started walking and showed her the way to the school of law building.

"Thank you, Professor," she said, pleased he had noticed.

He looked her up and down again. "You can't possibly want to do law. Come with me and you will not regret it. Law is ghastly; no one wants to do it. What can I do to change your mind? My office is just upstairs."

"Nice try, Professor." Sam stood her ground with both hands planted on her hips.

"Okay, okay, follow me. The law faculty is nearby, and I will introduce you to a wonderful colleague, Professor Alexander Grasim. Here he is. Alex, this is Sam. See if you can persuade her to change her mind. I told her that all of you in the law department are trouble and only I could give her a future that she deserves," he said in between a chuckle or two.

"Don't listen to him, Sam. He does this to all my students because he can't find enough for himself. Isn't that right, Professor Tenth?" said Professor Grasim.

"It's not too late. What do you say, Sam?" said Professor Tenth.

"It's law for me, sorry," Sam replied.

"Look after her, Alex!" Professor Tenth called out as he walked away.

"Will do, Ken," Professor Grasim replied. "Samantha Page, it that correct?" he asked while taking an envelope out of his jacket pocket. "Professor Tenth was kind enough to brief me about your aspirations and I put together an information package for you. The first semester of 2014 isn't until March, so you have plenty of time to look this over. I have included my contact details. Feel free to call me anytime. Enrolling can be very confusing. Professor Tenth told me where you work but do you have any tertiary or other qualifications?"

"No, none. Sorry," Sam replied without showing any disappointment and maintaining eye contact.

"That's fine. I covered that. It explains that you will need to fill out a prerequisite assessment. It is mostly based on maths, English and general knowledge. Plus, a short essay on your desired subject, yours being law, of course. It's designed for mature age students, like yourself, who wish to study but do not meet the admissions criteria because they don't have any qualifications and are not working within the sector. Do you understand?"

"Yes, thank you for meeting me and for putting this together for me."

"Well, it's up to you. You have certainly impressed

Professor Tenth, but you will need to do the hard work. Are you ready for it?"

"Yes, sir."

"See you next year, then, in the School of Law. The dates and times are all there for you. Good luck." He waved at her as he walked off.

Sam stood there for a minute or two before walking back out of the university. As she walked, she felt as if her feet weren't touching the ground. She was euphoric at the thought of having two professors interested in her and talking to her about her studies within the very grounds of the university. She was taking the next step and didn't plan to look back. Things were happening for her at an alarming pace and she owed it all to the book glasses.

Once out of the university grounds and into the adjacent park, guilt reared its ugly head and Sam was paralysed with fear.

Taking a seat on one of the many park benches, she was horrified to think she had somehow benefited from Mr Harman's death. This thought appalled her, and in her panic, she struggled to suck in a breath. To ease her breathing, she started taking rapid short breaths and was soon breathing normally, but the feeling was still there, and she didn't know how to deal with it.

Then it came to her that she was just as much a victim as poor Mr Harman. After all, she was just following his instructions. Since it was his last wish for her to take the glasses, she started feeling good about having them because that's what he would have wanted.

Her guilt dissolved, but the sadness lingered, and she felt more determined than ever to use the book glasses to help her achieve extraordinary heights.

She made her way to the refuge. She couldn't wait to tell Sue all about it.

"Sister Sue, I need to talk to you," Sam said in one puff of breath after running up to her.

"Wow, you look amazing, Sam. That business suit looks remarkable on you. That doesn't look like something from one of our bins. Did you steal it?" Sue asked.

"No, of course not. Can I talk to you in private, please?"

"Of course, let's go to my office," Sue said, pointing the way.

"Sister Sue, excuse me, ma'am. Oh, it's you, Sam. I didn't recognise you. Wow, you look fabulous!" said Sister Jan.

"Yes, what is it, Sister Jan?" Sister Sue asked.

"Nothing. It can keep for later. Lovely to see you, ma'am, I'm mean Sam." Sister Jan kept staring at Sam as she walked away.

Sam waved goodbye to her. "What's with her?"

"You, that's what with her. Come with me!" Sue said, a scowl pulling at her features.

Sue closed her office door behind them and sat behind her desk. "What's going on, Sam?"

"That's what I want to talk to you about. I've got a job and a boyfriend and I'm going to university next year. Can you believe it?"

"Honey, what are you talking about? How? Tell me from the start."

Sam felt it was time to tell someone and Sue had been there for her, right from when she'd first moved to Sydney over five years ago. She had helped her when she was alone and frightened in a new city with no friends, job, or family. If it hadn't been for Sue, Sam knew she would either be in jail or dead. She was indebted to her and felt it was time to return that trust and be open with her about what was happening in her life.

She began to tell her about Joyce, Mr Harman, the book glasses, Dr Julie Dunn, Billy, the two professors, even her winnings. She talked until Sue said she couldn't hear anymore and told her to stop.

The sister jumped out of her chair and walked out of her office. She soon returned with two glasses of water and after sitting back down, said, "The ghost-like images you described after wearing the glasses for more than five hours are dead people, you know. Lost souls walking around in purgatory. That's what you're seeing." She was shaking in fear and took a drink of water.

"How do you know?"

"It doesn't take an expert to figure it out. Tell me, why do you call them the book glasses?"

"Because that's when you get the full effect when reading a book. You don't get the full effect reading anything else."

"Give me some examples of what you mean by the full effect."

"Let's say I'm reading a book about prehistoric dinosaurs, then the drawings or pictures appear right in front of me in full-size 3D showing every detail and almost looking real. The words are also sent straight into my mind; I don't even need to read anything. They just appear in my mind and the difficult words are all explained in a way that makes it easy for me to remember. I'm able to remember and understand the content of all the books I read using the book glasses and I can read them at an incredible speed. I can get through a four-hundred-page book, on average, within an hour," Sam explained while taking the glasses case from her bag.

"Is that them?"

"Yes." She opened the case and placed them in the palm of her hand.

"I can see tiny writing up and down the frame both inside and out," Sue said.

"I've done some research. It's seventeenth-century neo-Latin. The engraving on the outside of the frames says, 'Commissioned by Pope Leo XIII, The Papal Basilica of St Peter, Rome.' And on the inside, 'The Holy Father's Book Glasses blessed by God, sent by angels for all imminent Popes.'"

"How can you read the frames while you have the glasses off?" Sue asked.

"I didn't. I have a mobile phone now and I took a photo of both the inside and outside of the frame and then I put the glasses back on to decipher them," Sam said with a grin.

"How did you come up with that idea and where did you learn to talk like that?" Sue looked terrified.

"I told you, it's the book glasses."

"Sam, they don't belong to you, they belong to the Catholic church. You must give them back," Sue said firmly.

A sense of betrayal settled over Sam. Return the glasses? "For the first time, I'm free from a lifetime of shackles that have been preventing me from doing what I want to do. My inabilities are no more, and you want me to give them back. You, of all people, should understand. How could you say that when I've been pouring my heart out to you every day for the past five years?

"You've seen how I've been living. I'm a twenty-three-year-old stupid, illiterate loser who has never had a boyfriend or a steady job or anything good happen in my life. Now I can read, there is a boy who is interested in me and may like me for me, and I have a chance to go to university and make something of myself."

Sam stood up. "But I guess you don't want that. You don't want me to succeed because you like having me around, don't you? Just in case a volunteer doesn't show up on a shift, you have me to take their place, don't you?"

Sue's eyes were stormy. "Are you finished? You sit back down and listen to me, young lady. Every time you cried because you didn't get a job, I cried right there with you. Whenever you felt terrified and alone, I was there next to you, feeling hopeful and blessed that you had entered my life. I'm a friend but I'm also a nun, sweetheart, and what you have there doesn't belong to you. They belong to the church and there's no escaping that. It's written on the frames; you said it yourself.

"You asked yourself why you can read suddenly, and why are all these things happening to you? What happens when bad things happen to you as a result of you having these glasses or, God forbid, also to other people? You are already seeing the dead. The glasses are sacred, and they belong to the church. Let's go and show Cardinal Graham together. The sooner you do this, the sooner you can get back to your life."

That was the last straw. Sam jumped up. "I knew it. You just want me back the way I was, your little helper, the loser who cleaned up all your shit. You haven't been listening at all. I've had enough of this bullshit. I'm going to have a boyfriend and go to university and make something of my life. I'm getting out of here!" Sam stormed out the office, slamming the door behind her.

———

Alone in her empty office, Sue feared that her worst nightmare, of losing Sam forever, had finally come true. From the first day she'd walked into her office, five years before, vulnerable and scared, Sue had been fearing this. And she was still too afraid to tell her the truth about who she was. If it hadn't been for Joyce, she would have done it long ago.

"Hello, Sister Sue, I'm Samantha Page. They told me to see you about doing some volunteering here while I'm looking for a job," Sam said politely after closing the door behind her.

"Yes, please come in and take a seat." Sue was almost breathless with shock to see how beautiful Samantha was. She had been told the day before that a Samantha Page wanted to see her, and she and Joyce had both agreed that it had to be her Sam.

"Where did you move from Sam? Can I call you Sam?" Sue said with a smile.

"Yes, you can call me Sam. I moved from Melbourne last week, but I don't want to talk about that please." She folded her arms across her chest.

"Okay, that's fine. What sort of job are you looking for?" Sue settled back down and managed to keep her nerves under control.

"Anything with my hands. Nothing where I would need to read."

"I see. Any reason for that?"

"Reading is a problem. I have dyslexia," Sam explained.

"Everyone has something they struggle with. Don't let that stop you chasing your dreams, okay?"

"Can you give me a reference for a job, please?" Sam asked.

"I need to get to know you first. Would you like to help us out here from time to time? If you do, I would be happy to give you a reference."

"Yeah, okay." Sam smiled.

After Sam left, Sue returned to her office, and gave in to her tears. She phoned Joyce, who said she'd come immediately.

Her baby was a slim five-foot-seven-inch beauty with light blue eyes and gorgeous long brown hair. Although she had done her best to hide the cuts up and down her arms, they were as clear as day to Sue, all too familiar with seeing the damage left behind by child abuse and bullies over the years. She blamed *herself for putting Sam in that situation and was filled with anguish.*

"Hey, enough of that. You need to be strong for your girl, honey," Joyce said softly as she came in and embraced Sue.

"Joyce, my baby was abused and it's my fault!"

"Look, we can't do anything about the past, but we can do something from now on."

"I guess," Sue said as she tried her best not to cry again. "I don't know what to do."

"If we tell her who we are now she will go away and not come back. She's eighteen years old and full of anger. Do you remember when we were eighteen? We need to be cool and let her settle in first. If she volunteers here, you can establish a trusting relationship and then tell her when the time is right. In the meantime, you can help her find a job and help her with her needs. Here's your chance to protect her, honey. That's what you want, isn't it?" "But if I don't go to her now, when she finds out she won't forgive me."

But Joyce had worried that it would be too much for Sam, that she would leave, and they would never see her again. Sue had listened and done as she'd said, and, as she'd expected, every day that passed it became harder to tell Sam the truth.

It was all too much for her. She did not have the strength to fight her fear of losing Sam. All she could do was respect her wishes to keep the book glasses, despite how strongly she felt about what they could do to her.

FIRST OFFICIAL DATE

Furious at Sue for trying to take her new life away from her, Sam ran all the way home, vowing never to go back to the refuge or see her again.

She had everything under control. All she needed to remember was never to overuse the book glasses and never to tell anyone else about them. Revealing the secret to Sue had been a mistake. Nor would she leave evidence for anyone visiting from the refuge to suspect she was reading. She collected all the books scattered around her apartment and took them back to the library.

While she was there, Sam received a text message but left it unread. As soon as she got home, she put on the glasses and found the message was from Billy. He said he couldn't wait until Saturday to see her and asked her to meet him for dinner the following day, Friday at 6:30 p.m. near her place in the city.

Thrilled, Sam quickly replied she would like to leave it as they planned for Saturday and assured him the wait would be worth it.

It would be their first official date. Never before had she

connected with someone so quickly. It was almost like a dream and yet it was real. Thinking of his smile and the way he had looked after her warmed her heart. She couldn't wait to see him again!

She wondered where Billy would take her on Saturday. *What will I wear?* she thought. *I can't wear the same black dress I wore last week.* Remembering it was Thursday night, she decided to go shopping.

Why not? she asked herself, *I have money.* "I'm going shopping!" she declared to her empty apartment.

Then another daring idea popped into her mind. Instead of takeaway, she would eat out in a real restaurant. A restaurant with waiters and wine and silver cutlery. She would use it as a practice run so she wouldn't embarrass poor Billy at dinner.

She carefully stowed the glasses in her bag and headed off on her adventure. First stop was to buy a dress, shoes, and accessories to wear on her date. With her glasses by her side, she had all the confidence she needed to make her outing a success.

For the first hour, she looked around to find out what was fashionable and compare prices. Although money wasn't an issue now, she knew she wanted a bargain and finding it was going to be fun.

Four hours later, Sam returned to a dark apartment and dropped all her shopping onto her bed; a bed desperately in need of a new mattress.

As usual, her first thought was to take care of the book glasses. She took them off and secured them in her bag, which she hid in her closet.

She couldn't wait to open all her shopping bags to look at what she had bought. After unpacking all the bags and spreading all her purchases out on her bed, she was in awe.

The blue sleeveless dress that highlighted her blue eyes,

along with matching shoes, was a magnificent choice but she felt the five-hundred-dollar Saint Laurent clutch purse was a little excessive. She was glad she had shrewdly sidestepped the jewellery department, fearing a further cost blowout. And while City Quay at Circular Quay was far from fine dining, eating there had been a dream come true for Sam after walking past the restaurant for five years.

Over dinner, she had decided she would need a lot more money to live on; much more than she'd won at the casino because the glasses would always opt for quality over price. It was amazing to recall that only weeks ago she could barely pay her rent, most days she had eaten all her meals at the refuge because she couldn't afford to buy food, and her wardrobe had consisted of second-hand clothes from a charity clothing bin.

That night she went to sleep dreaming of restaurants and ferries, wharves and water. In particular, she dreamed about City Quay, the delightful harbour view restaurant overlooking Circular Quay wharves, where she would meet Billy the following day.

Sam woke with a start on Saturday morning, ate breakfast in haste and opened her new portmanteau case of brand-new makeup specifically designed for her. After the previous night's preparations, she was ready for her first date.

For a small fortune, a professional department store makeup artist had filled the case with an array of designer label makeup and application paraphernalia that would bring a smile to Oprah Winfrey.

Once she had applied her makeup, the result was so astonishing that she couldn't tell if it was her skills or the superior quality of the products. If her lipstick hadn't been so glamorous, no one would have been able to tell she had any makeup on at all.

With only minutes to spare, Sam finished getting dressed and took off out the door after grabbing her black bag and putting it on her chest backwards. She always strove to keep the book glasses safe and secure and never out of reach. After all, this would be her first official date with a boy, and she needed the glasses close by just in case things started going wrong. It was reassuring to know she had them ready to back her up at a moment's notice.

With an hour to get to Manly Wharf, as she waited for her ferry, Sam watched the other ferries come and go from Circular Quay wharf number three. The sun was the colour of her orange-red lipstick in a cloudless sky and the sea breeze played havoc with her ocean-coloured dress, repeatedly teasing the hem, and lifting her skirt.

Overwhelmed with joy and happiness at the thought of seeing Billy again, Sam's heart leapt in her chest. She couldn't wait to be in arms again to confirm that he and her feelings for him were real.

On the ferry ride, her mind was so filled with dreams and possibilities that she barely noticed the view and was surprised when the ferry docked. She stepped off onto Manly Wharf and Billy surprised her by coming up from behind her and greeting her with a hug. She quickly turned around and hugged him even tighter.

"I'm here early. What are you doing here?" Sam said with a huge smile.

"Are you kidding? I've been here since 10a.m., waiting for you. I've had so many coffees I'm starting to talk fast," Billy said.

After another long hug and an even longer kiss, they walked

off hand in hand, talking about their week. She admired his navy shorts and his half-open shirt with tropical fish on an ocean blue background that matched her dress. Their sandals were almost the same too and she loved that he looked much taller than he had last time when she'd been wearing heels. He was everything she had wished for and more. He was gentle and polite and always asked her how she felt about things before doing anything.

"You know, we did go out together last week but really, today is our first official date," Billy said.

"Yes, I know," Sam said, concealing the fact her heart was rapidly fluttering as she realised he felt the same about her as she did about him.

"After a light lunch on the beach, I've organised a mini-bus tour around Manly. You are going to love it. My mate, Tony, who runs a local travel agency, has arranged an afternoon of sightseeing. It's a private tour just for the two of us. How about that?

"But that's not all, I've also booked a table for dinner in a seafood restaurant overlooking the water. What do you think, Sam, happy with that?" he asked with arms open, waiting for a response.

"Thank you, that sounds wonderful," she said with a smile, then jumped into his arms.

"Here, look at the itinerary for our mini-bus." He was so excited, he practically positioned it right in front of her face and started reading it aloud, "We are going to Manly, Balgo-wlah, Seaforth, Curl Curl, Dee Why, Collaroy, Long Reef, Narrabeen, Warriewood, Mona Vale, Newport, Bilgola, Akuna Bay, Avalon, Careel Bay, Palm Beach and back to Manly!" She confirmed how happy she was with a quick kiss.

From then on, it was a whirlwind of fun, adventure, and amazing food. Billy had organised the day so well that Sam's feet hardly touched the ground as she was whisked away by the man of her dreams.

After dessert at the Manly seaside restaurant that night, Sam paused, looked at Billy and didn't think things could get any better. Then he invited her back to his place. Without hesitation, she nodded, and her smile lit up the entire restaurant.

MAKING MORE MONEY

"Billy? Are you there?" Sam called out after waking up naked in Billy's bed with no sign of him.

"It's okay, Sam. I'm making breakfast for us. Go ahead and have a shower and breakfast will be ready by the time you finish," Billy replied from the kitchen.

Freshly showered and wearing only one of Billy's white t-shirts that she had pulled out of his cupboard, she followed the noise to the kitchen.

Their entire morning was filled with laughter and conversation. They constantly touched each another and talked about their lives and everything else, while feasting on an assortment of bacon and eggs, pancakes, and fruit salad.

Once they'd cleaned up from breakfast, they settled back into the bedroom and talked some more. It was the perfect relaxed morning.

They had been talking almost nonstop for a few hours, wrapped in each other arms in his bed, when Billy mentioned that one day, he would like to travel all over Australia. Sam jumped up and told him that this had been her dream since coming to Sydney. She was beside herself and Billy's eyes just kept widening the more Sam shared about her hopes and dreams. Their cuddles soon turned into an afternoon full of passionate lovemaking.

Their love was real, but for Sam, it was a lot more than that because this day had washed away all the years of solitude and the tears she had shed alone. Afterwards, she held Billy so tightly and knew he wasn't just her first love, but he would be her forever love.

Dinner at a fashionable Italian restaurant back in the city completed a wonderful and memorable weekend for Sam. By the time Billy walked her home, both were content to part ways, if only for a short period.

The following Saturday felt a world away and they settled on promising to call each other daily. Before one last kiss good-night, Sam invited him to stay at her place next week and he was overjoyed to accept.

Her feet didn't even touch the floor when she walked into her apartment. Feeling lightheaded with love, she paused for a minute or two, thinking it was all a dream.

But Billy wasn't a dream. He was a magnanimous spirit who was very real who loved her as much as she loved him.

She went about getting ready for bed, dancing and singing unashamedly around her apartment before settling down.

———

The next morning her phone buzzed and woke her, prompting Sam to read Billy's good morning text which elicited smiles and laughter.

She relished the thought of having someone who cared about her and was interested in every part of her life. Feeling this way was strange and new but she cherished every single moment.

As she placed the phone back down on the bedside table, took off the book glasses and put them in their case, she contemplated that she'd had the weekend of a lifetime without the book glasses. She hadn't put them on once.

This struck a deep chord in Sam, who concluded that Billy loved her for her and not because of anything she had concocted with the assistance of the glasses. This revelation filled her heart with contentment and a sense of fulfilment beyond belief.

It was during her morning shower, still high on these blissful feelings, that Sam determined what to do next. She was ready to take on the challenge of making more money.

The casino was not on her agenda that day. Instead, she deliberated on the content of her reading matter from the week before. She had read through an array of economics books as well as *Australian Financial Review* newspapers from the last few weeks.

She had five thousand dollars of her winnings left. The stock market had attracted her interest with a potential return on investment that the casino's odds could not match.

She was excited about the possibilities of the stock market, because, although general confidence was at an all-time low, the newspaper articles reflected the opposite for a select number of high-profile corporations, with their CEO bonuses at an all-time high and huge quarterly profits, giving conflicting reports of the current financial situation.

Instinctively, she knew she could capitalise on this in the short term by selectively investing in these businesses before other investors jumped on the bandwagon and tipped the scales of profit.

She quickly dressed in her business suit and applied her

makeup while wearing the book glasses and was out the door in no time, looking fabulous.

It was Monday morning and she intended to infiltrate a nearby investment company. She didn't want to ring around for vacant positions within these companies or wait on the phone or arrange interviews. Instead, she would walk into an investment job by using her own money to prove to her employer that she had the skills and the talent to make money on the stock market.

———

"Sam, I would like you to stay on? What will it take for you to continue working here at Mercantile Investment Group? The last two months have been memorable! You have done what you set out to do and then some. You've impressed us all, so stop and think about what you are doing."

The entire senior staff who were gathered in the boardroom waited in silence for Sam's response as the CEO sat back down in his chair.

"Thank you, Isaac. You are too kind, but I told you from the beginning that I would be here only for a couple of months," she explained, looking around at all the shocked faces.

"Our senior team has watched you and your predictions and, like you, they have been faultless. You have the uncanny ability to select stock at the right time with flair and know how the likes of which we have never seen before. I would like to offer you a senior partnership with full shares in the business. What do you say now—senior partner and full shares?" Isaac looked hopeful.

"I'm flattered, Isaac, and it's been an honour. You have my deepest respect and I'm sure you will take the company to much greater heights without me," she replied with a sincere smile.

"I'm never going to stop trying. I'll transfer your earnings into your account plus a ten percent bonus at the end of trade today. Just remember, as long as I'm here, you will always have a job," Isaac said, his crestfallen expression nagging at Sam.

With a nod of her head, she was out the door and raced down the corridor to the toilets. Once in the privacy of a toilet cubical, she quickly took off the book glasses and hid them in her bra before collapsing onto the closed lid of the toilet seat.

Fainting had become a regular occurrence as a result of wearing the book glasses for eight hours or more each day. Knowing she was unable to sustain this for much longer had made it easier for Sam to quit her financially rewarding investment job after only two months.

Blocking out the frightening ghost-like figures that appeared after she'd worn the glasses for more than five hours was manageable to a point, but the associated headaches became unbearable from the eight-hour mark onward.

Aware that her every move was being watched the entire time she was at work and every phone call was recorded, analysed, and scrutinised, she needed to keep the glasses on at all times. Yet, she could not afford to attract any attention to them and refused to enter into any conversation about the glasses, leaving everyone to speculate that her eccentric tastes were behind their unique design.

The sound of the toilet flushing in the next cubical brought some life back into her. She waited until the bathroom was empty before going out and washing her face with cold water. With the book glasses still nestled in her bra, she took off home with her head thumping. She barely made it into her bedroom before she collapsed onto her bed fully dressed.

She slept through until the next morning, waking up when

her phone buzzed. Thinking it was her usual endearing morning text from Billy as she reached out onto the bedside table to search for her glasses, she was shocked to find them still in her bra. Immediately, she remembered the events of the previous day and how she had finished up at her investment job.

She jumped out of bed, put on the glasses, and took out her laptop. When she logged into her online banking, she was pleasantly surprised to see a balance of over two point two million dollars in her account.

Setting out to do this over two months was one thing, but she'd had no idea she could turn her five thousand dollars into two point two million dollars in such a short time.

She tossed the laptop back on the bed and tears of joy and happiness rolled down her face.

TWENTY-FIVE PERCENT

"Billy, stop that. I love you so don't compare me with your ex-girlfriend. Going to university is not about you, it's about me and I need your support to do it. It's a big step for me and I don't think I can do it without you. I didn't even finish high school, for goodness' sake, and I'm afraid. But I know that if I do this and, if it doesn't work out, then I still have you. I know you're afraid, but so am I," Sam said.

"You haven't finished high school and yet you got into a law degree at one of the most prestigious universities in the country. How does that happen?" Billy asked.

"I've been working on this for years. I'm not going to uni to pick up men. I'm not interested in anyone else. I love you!" Sam yelled back.

"Okay, okay. I love you too. Does this mean we've just had our first fight?" Billy said and started to laugh.

"You really are a dick, you know," said Sam and fell into his arms. "I took the mature age entry test last Monday and they informed me yesterday that I was successful. I got the highest test result any mature age student has ever received, so how about that?"

"I'm proud of you. Sorry, Sam, but when you told me you sat for a test to get into a law degree at of all places, Sydney University, and you got in, that freaked me out. I didn't expect that you of all people would do that to me. All I was thinking about is what kind of new boyfriend you're going to find at uni. I fucking hate universities, all they do is fucking go at it like rabbits. There is so much sex going on it's amazing anyone graduates."

"Now that's an idea. I'd never thought of that." Sam giggled.

"Don't you dare. I couldn't deal with it happening to me a second time," Billy said, looking into her eyes.

"I love you, you crazy guy. I will never leave you now that I've found you." Sam gave him a tender kiss.

The kisses continued into Billy's bedroom and they forgot about the Chinese takeaway that had just been delivered, opting to make love instead. The food was just starting to cool when they took to it like starving hyenas, much in need of nourishment after their tiresome exchange and their makeup sex.

"I've decided to take a room at the university dorms accommodation; a tiny studio apartment. It's for studying and sleeping only so that means we'll be at your place every weekend. Is that okay?" Sam asked with a mouthful of noodles.

"Well, that's what I was going to talk to you about," Billy mumbled through a mouth even more full of food than hers.

"Yeah, what?" Sam stopped eating.

Billy swallowed his mouthful. "This apartment is up for sale and I've got four weeks to get out. Sorry, Sam. I'm nowhere near close to having the deposit to buy it like I'd always planned."

"Is that all? No worries. How much do you need for the deposit?" She took another mouthful.

"Ha, ha. That's a good one. Stop joking around, I'm serious."

"Look, I know how much you love the place and that you can go surfing anytime you like because it's so close to the beach. So how much you need for the deposit?"

"You're not joking, are you?"

"No, I'm not. How much?"

"One hundred and twenty thousand dollars. It's twenty-five percent of the asking price, which is four hundred and eighty thousand."

"Fine."

"What do you mean fine? Where are you going to find one hundred and twenty thousand dollars to give me? Are you going to rob a bank or something?" Billy joked.

"I have some savings so let me do this for you, please. What yours is mine and what's mine is yours anyway, so what's the problem? But you are the one getting the home loan, so you'll need to move fast. I'll transfer you the money tonight after you take me home, okay?"

Sam resumed eating as Billy sat back in the lounge, speechless. She spent the rest of the night convincing him to take the money and by the time they got to her apartment, it was finally settled.

While Billy was in the bathroom, she put on the book glasses and transferred the money. Still wearing the glasses, Sam wrote a set of instructions and warnings about what bank and home loan to select, what was an accessible interest rate, which home conveyancing to use and when to inform the owner's real estate agent of his offer.

When she heard him coming, she slipped off the glasses and put them back in her bag, before turning and handing him the note. "Here are some instructions on what you need to do for the home loan. The most important is not to accept the sale price until you've exhausted negotiating the price down as much as possible. Then, once you've got their bottom price, negotiate it down further. I've transferred the entire amount into your account."

He looked confused. "Why did you transfer the whole amount if I'm going to negotiate the price down?"

She shrugged. "If someone else is interested in buying the property, you may need to pay the full price to get it. That's the worst-case scenario, but it could happen, so you need to be ready for it."

Billy stared at her with his mouth hanging open. "I guess you do belong at university!"

With the set of instructions in his pocket and the deposit in his bank account, he wished her well for her first day at university with a passionate kiss and a huge hug. He then headed back to his apartment, looking as happy as she'd ever seen him.

WELCOME TO SYDNEY UNIVERSITY

3rd March 2014

As Sam walked into the crowded auditorium, she tried not to feel overwhelmed. It was Orientation Day at Sydney University, and it was easy to feel awed as she looked at the students milling around. She was sure all of them had finished high school, probably passing with the highest marks in their classes.

She found a seat at the back, trying to blend in.

Within a few minutes, Professor Grasim went to the lectern at the front of the hall. He waited until silence fell, then began to speak.

"Good morning all and welcome to Sydney University Law Faculty undergraduate intake for 2014. My name is Professor Alexander Grasim.

"On average, students doing a double degree full time will take six years to complete it. A double degree is now the standard. The most common double degree combinations are law and arts or law and business. However, there are many choices, and the choice is yours.

"Whether you do a law degree only or a double degree, it is up to you. But remember, you have only four weeks from today to make your selection, so select wisely because after that you're paying for it."

A murmur of conversation ran throughout the auditorium.

The professor frowned. "Pay attention, people. On the screens behind me, I have put up our marking criteria: high distinction, eighty-five to one hundred percent. Distinction, seventy-five to eighty-four percent. Credit, sixty-five to seventy-four percent, Pass, fifty to sixty-four percent. Fail, zero to forty-nine percent.

"For those students who think that passes mean degrees, I'm sorry to say, you are at the wrong university. Here, we strive for excellence and I have a formula for those undergrads interested in exceeding expectations within the law faculty."

The rumble of conversation began to rise again before the professor silenced it with a look. "So, listen up, everyone, you don't want to miss this. All you need to do is to follow these three steps.

"One—attend all classes, both lectures and tutorials. Although online resources are available to every student, by attending all classes, you will benefit from the interactions with your fellow students, lecturers, and tutors.

"Two—participate in all classroom, lecture and online activities. Don't underestimate the value of these activities. And everything adds up to your overall total mark.

"Three—do the minimum readings. I am always amazed at how unprepared many students are, coming into class without doing this.

"Following those three steps will give you a pass, but a pass is not what we aim to produce here at Sydney University. We aim to produce excellence. To achieve excellence, you need to make sure your essays and papers are handed in on time. What is not expected is that you leave them to the last minute.

"When I mark undergrad essays or papers, I look at the student's name first for two reasons: one—if they do not do well and have completed the three steps I have outlined, it may be enough to tip them over to a pass. Two—if they do not do well and have booked a meeting with me about it or have approached me in class, it may also be enough to tip them over to a pass.

"Never leave your essays or papers to the last minute. To set yourself up for excellence, you must arrange a meeting with your professor first to see if you are on the right track at least two weeks before the assessment is due.

"I would like to take this opportunity to wish you success in your studies."

Applause erupted from the crowded auditorium and the professor held up his hand for silence. "Thank you, but I'm not finished. Quiet, please. Every year, we have a large intake of mature age students whose acceptance is based on an entry exam and we acknowledge the student with the highest entry exam mark with an award. This year, I'm proud to announce the mature age student with the highest entry exam mark in the history of the university is twenty-three-year-old Samantha Page. Please give her a round of applause."

When Sam stood up from her seat, the roar of the crowd was deafening. Accepting this award didn't sit right with her. It felt almost fraudulent, but she plastered a smile on her face and walked up onto the stage anyway.

The professor stepped away from the lectern, showing a plaque displaying her perfect score. "Congratulations, Samantha Page. We are all expecting great things from you."

After shaking hands with the various faculty members on

the stage, she followed the crowd of students to the administration building to pick her four units for the first semester. To lay the foundation for a double degree in law and economics, she chose two law units and two economics units.

At the cafeteria at lunchtime, when a dozen or more new undergrads from all walks of life gathered around her to congratulate her on her award, she quickly lost her appetite. Reluctantly, she answered their questions, keeping her answers vague yet interesting. Despite feeling like a fraud, she enjoyed the attention and was soon caught up in the whirlwind of excitement as she looked around at all the keen smiling faces.

Looking into their eyes, Sam saw glimpses of uncertainty and even despair in many of them; emotions she was all too familiar with, but she was finally free of that doubt and hopelessness.

"We're off to sign up at the library. Would you like to come with us?" asked one student.

"Sure," said Sam. No longer hungry, she wrapped up her half-eaten sandwich, placed it in her bag and followed the group of students to the university library.

She took two steps into the magnificent building and stood there in awe. As the other students lined up at the front desk, Sam walked up and down the aisles with her arms stretched out, gently gliding her fingers over the books on the shelves. She put on the book glasses to find the first two books on her reading list—one law and one economics text—and took a seat and started reading them.

Almost zombie-like, she consumed them, the books taking her to a place she had never been before. By the time she had finished them both, the front desk was clear of students and she hurried to sign up, quickly arranging to borrow the two books before anyone else noticed she had them.

Keeping the book glasses on for the rest of the day, Sam was in her element and, by that afternoon, to her delight and relief, no one had questioned her about them. The university tour had satisfied her appetite for antiquity and, after enjoying some refreshments, she left the other students to pick up her award from the professor's office.

"Come in, Samantha." Professor Grasim stood up from behind his desk.

"Thank you, Professor."

"Those glasses are exceptional. Where did you get them?"

It was unsettling to see the way his eyes examined them. "These old things? They are a family hand-me-down that I got new lenses for," she replied, trying to cover them with her hands.

"They're unusual, aren't they? They look very old."

Sam changed the subject as she took off the glasses and swiftly placed them in her shoulder bag. "Thank you for holding onto my award, Professor. I'm still so shocked and also very honoured."

"The university and I are honoured to have you. How did you find the tour?"

"It was great, thanks. A lot to take in all in one day."

"Good. Is there anything I can help you with in enrolment or anything else?"

"Well, there is something I'm not quite sure how to go about, actually."

"If I can help, I will be happy to do so."

"I don't know how to go about arranging university dorm accommodation. If you could tell me who to talk to it would be a great help."

"Leave that up to me. I'll get administration to email you all the arrangements. I have your email address. It will be my pleasure, but I need to warn you, it is expensive."

"Wow, thank you. I don't know what to say." She got up from her chair.

"We just need you to do your best, Sam. Congratulations once again. Remember, my door is always open. Good luck." The professor handed her the award and walked her out of his office.

LANGUAGES

7th June 2014

"*Ciao, vorremmo una bottiglia del tuo buon vino rosso con il nostro pane all'aglio. Inoltre, siamo pronti per ordinare la nostra alimentazione, due spaghetti marineras. Questo è tutto grazie,*" Sam said with a smile and handed both menus back to the waiter.

"*Grazie, un minute.*"

"Wow, you didn't tell me you could speak Italian. You are amazing, Samantha Page. So, what did you say to the waiter? All I heard was spaghetti marinara."

"Yes, I just ordered that for our mains, plus garlic bread for entrée and a bottle of their good red wine. That's it," Sam said.

"Who are you?" Billy whispered.

"Wouldn't you like to know?" Sam whispered back and they burst into laughter. "I'm learning French at the moment."

But Billy's face became serious. "Look, sorry to put a damper on things but since you started uni, I've hardly spent any time with you. The few nights we've had together at my place is not my idea of a relationship. Now you're telling me you're learning languages as well? No wonder you don't have any time for me." He folded his arms across his chest.

"I'm sorry, honey, but you did tell me I have your support. You know what this means to me," Sam said as the waiter opened the bottle of red wine and poured two glasses.

He sighed. "I'm sorry too, sweetheart, I don't know what got into me. Things are getting hectic for me and the stress is wearing me down."

"What's happening? It's not about your apartment, is it?"

"No, everything is fine. My loan came through and I've purchased it. Because you gave me the deposit, I made sure I put both of our names on the title," he announced with a huge smile.

"You didn't need to do that."

"Yes, I did, because I love you." He picked up his glass of wine and kept looking at her as they both took their first drink.

"So, what's worrying you, honey?" Sam asked.

"Nothing. Don't worry about it. I'm sorry I said anything."

"Look, you'd better tell me. I need to know because I love you."

"Okay, here it is. When I'm stressed and alone, I go to the casino and gamble. I've been so worried about my parents since they split up and even though they're back together and in counselling now, I keep worrying about them.

"And since you've been away, I haven't been able to handle the empty apartment, so I've been going to the casino every night. I didn't want to touch my wages and risk missing mortgage repayments, so I borrowed some money from a loan shark and I'm now in the hole with him for one hundred and fifty Gs." Billy looked down at the table, unable to meet her eyes.

"Do you mean one hundred and fifty thousand dollars?" Sam asked in shock.

"Yes. When I lost the first amount I borrowed, I thought that I could somehow win and pay him off, so I borrowed more. I did win some of it back, but I ended up gambling that too. Now he has cut me off and given me seven days to come up with the money or else," Billy said while refilling his glass.

"Or else what? Is he going to break your legs or something?"

"No, he wants the deed to the apartment, or he will kill me if I don't come up with the money within a week." There were tears in his eyes.

Her heart broke for him. "Billy, you're smarter than this. I told you that I'm yours—I'm not going anywhere—and it sounds like your parents are working things out, so why are you stressed? I suspect it's just an excuse because you have an addiction to gambling, don't you? You didn't just meet this loan shark recently, not if you're in for that much money. You've been doing this for a while and that's why your previous girl-friend left you, isn't it?"

He looked crestfallen. "Yes, you're right, I do have a gambling addiction and I've been borrowing money for over a year, but my ex didn't leave me because of my gambling. She left me because she slept with practically every student in her class and got pregnant to one of them. I'm sorry, sweetheart, yes, I'm a gambler. You're right."

She took his hand. "It's okay, honey. We can work it out. Thank you for admitting it. But let's not worry about that now and just enjoy this wonderful dinner, okay?" Sam picked up her glass of wine. "*Saluti!*"

"*Saluti?* What's that?" he asked, puzzled.

"It means 'cheers' in Italian," Sam clarified with a smile.

Their food was served, and they ate as if Billy hadn't mentioned his dilemma. With every mouthful, she could see him watching her as if he was waiting for her to explode, but she just enjoyed the moment and the exceptional food while occasionally glancing over at him with a smile.

Sam didn't care about the money nor was she overly worried about the danger he was in. As long as she had the book glasses, she knew all that could be worked out. She loved the fact he had been honest with her about his gambling problem and did feel a little guilty about leaving him alone so much since starting uni. Unfortunately, she knew his gambling addiction was something she couldn't fix.

When they walked out of the seaside restaurant, they were greeted by the reflection of the full moon on the ocean and opted for a stroll along Manly Beach. A light breeze played with the tips of the waves and as they walked in the moonlight hand in hand. Occasionally, they would stop for a kiss before continuing as if they didn't have a care in the world. Eventually, they took a seat on a bench to take in the view in silence.

Sam turned to him. "Billy, this is what is going to happen. We will both go back to the casino one last time and win that money to pay off the loan shark. You need to trust me that we can do this. But if we do this, you need to promise me you will get help for your gambling addiction. Also, you must never go to the casino again or borrow money from anyone. If you love me, please agree to this."

From the look he gave her, she could tell he wasn't convinced. "Yes, and I do love you, but we are talking about one hundred and fifty thousand dollars, sweetheart. How are we going to win that much? I've been going to the casino for years and have never seen anyone win anywhere near that much money."

"That's because you haven't had access to the high roller room, exclusive to elite players," Sam replied with a grin.

"There is a reason for that. Anyway, how do you know about the high roller room? You don't gamble. When I took you to the casino, didn't you tell me you had never been in a casino before?"

"Check this out, honey." She handed him a business card.

"Frederick Hans, Casino Manager, VIP Premium Specialist," he read, his eyes popping wide open. "Who are you? Are you a secret agent and you're not telling me?"

Sam laughed. "Don't be silly. Are we going to do this or what?" She took back the card and placed it in her purse.

"Yes, of course, but I don't need to tell you that I'm a bad gambler. I'm hopeless. How are we going to win that much money even if we get into the high roller room with your friend's help?" Billy looked dejected.

"Frederick is not my friend. He was the one who personally invited me to the high roller room after discovering I had just won ten thousand dollars. It was amazing! They gave me an array of expensive gifts and complimentary drinks and food. They really look after their high rollers."

"Ten thousand dollars? What? How? When?" He sat there in disbelief.

"Never mind about that. Just trust me, honey, please. It's best I leave out the details for our safety. Tomorrow is Sunday, so how about we have dinner first before making our way to the high roller room? That gives us five days to win the entire amount, so even if we have a bad day, we still have plenty of time to get the one hundred and fifty thousand dollars before next Saturday."

He took her hands, gazing deep into her eyes. "I promise I won't ever disappoint you again. I will get help with the gambling. I would do anything for you. I know I want to be with you forever, and I couldn't recover if I ever lost you. You are the love of my life."

Her heart swelled at his words and she leant forward, holding him close and kissing him. "And you are mine."

THREE MEN

The next day, Billy came over early to help Sam move out of her apartment and into her university accommodation. She was not disappointed to leave that horrid place. She was jumping up and down with joy and had already packed all her possessions in boxes weeks earlier and cleaned the apartment from top to bottom.

The real estate agent had been notified and the vacancy papers had been signed with notice given in advance of this glorious day. All they needed to do was transport the boxes in the trailer Billy had hired.

Although things were right on schedule, Sam suddenly had a sickening feeling that she had not told Sue, or anyone from the refuge, that she was moving out. Feeling like that part of her life was behind her, she didn't want to open any wounds, nor did she think she needed to explain her decisions to anyone. She was tired of feeling that way and was determined that no one was going to tell her what to do ever again.

But, to her surprise, the feeling worsened as the day progressed.

"I love your little place here, sweetheart. It's a bit small, but how good is it being able to live on the university grounds? That's awesome!" Billy said, breathing heavily after carrying another box into the studio apartment.

"I know. I'm so excited about being here, honey." Sam kissed him.

"If you run into my ex, tell her she did me a favour by breaking up with me," Billy said, flipping the bird.

"Didn't you say she was pregnant?" Sam asked as she walked into the tiny kitchenette.

"Yes, but I think she's still attending classes, even though she'd be *very* pregnant by now."

"She'll be easy to spot, then," she said with a giggle.

"I just need to pick up one last load. So how about you stay here and unpack while I go back and get the last few boxes?"

"Thanks, honey. That would be great." She kissed him and went back to her unpacking.

———

Billy had just put the last box in the trailer when a black van stopped behind him with three men in it. They waited and watched him for a minute or two before the driver stepped out and approached him. "Excuse me, son, do you know where Samantha Page lives?"

Billy was startled by the man's appearance. The look was all too familiar from his recent dealings with the loan shark. The scars on his face and his aggressive stance painted a clear picture of the sort of man he was. And who wore a jacket on a hot summer's day? Billy was pretty sure he was concealing a weapon, just as the loan shark heavies had when they'd approached him.

"Samantha who?" he said.

"Samantha Page. I have a package to deliver to her," the thug said impatiently.

"No, sorry. I don't know anyone by that name. I'm just moving out of here myself after a short stay so I can't help you," Billy replied without faltering.

"Okay, kid. Thanks." As he walked into the building, Billy noticed a bulge in the shape of a gun under his jacket.

Billy tied up the last of the boxes, relieved he had already locked Sam's apartment and didn't need to go back in. While the thug was still inside asking around, he quickly drove off. Although fairly sure he wasn't being followed, he took the long route back to the university and kept his eyes on the rearview mirror. All the way, he wondered why people like that would be asking after his Sam.

After ensuring no one was following him, he drove into the university grounds, parked, and ran to her unit. "Sam, guess what happened?"

"What happened? Are you all right?" Sam asked.

"After locking up your apartment up, I was tying down the boxes in the trailer when three men in a black van stopped directly behind me. The driver got out and asked if I knew a Samantha Page."

"Did you say three men?" Sam asked with a quiver in her voice.

"Yes, three men in a black van."

"What did you tell them?" There was fear in her eyes.

"I said I didn't know anyone by that name and told them I was moving out after a short stay. I made sure I wasn't followed."

She looked unsettled. "Why? How did you know to do that?"

"It was easy. They looked like the thugs who work for the loan shark and immediately I knew something was wrong."

Billy noticed the change in her face. It confirmed his speculations. "There was no way I wanted them going anywhere near you."

"Thank you, honey. You are fantastic." She threw her arms around him.

After holding her for a minute, he drew away, taking her hands in his. "Why are people like that after you, sweetheart? And don't give me the 'trust me' bullshit. You need to tell me just like I told you about my gambling problem, okay? We need to start being honest with each other."

To his relief, she agreed. "You're right, sweetheart, but you need to first understand that by not telling you, if they ever talked to you, they would know you didn't know about it. All I was doing was keeping you out of harm's way."

"Know about what?" Billy asked. He firmly gripped her face with both hands and looked into her eyes.

"The book glasses. It's all about the book glasses," Sam finally said, her eyes filling with tears. "If anything happens to you, my love, I don't know what I will do. I've had too much disappointment in my life."

The book glasses? What book glasses? The fear on his face made him hold her tighter. "I've never seen you like this. Nothing will happen, sweetheart. Don't worry, okay? Are you all right?" After another hug and a kiss, he looked at her. "What are the book glasses, Sam?"

"Back while I was working at the museum, the CEO Mr Harman, with his last dying breath, gave the book glasses to me and made me promise not to tell anyone about them."

"Why was he dying? Was he ill?"

The tears traced her cheeks. "No, he was murdered. Three men killed him. They stabbed him and left him for dead in his office. They were looking for the book glasses. I think the three men you saw were the ones who killed him and now they're looking for me."

"How do you know all this?" Billy was almost afraid to hear her answer.

"After leaving him for dead, they brushed by me in the hallway as they took off. I ran into Mr Harman's office to find him on the floor with a knife sticking out of his chest. He told me where he had hidden the book glasses and made me promise I would never tell anyone that I had them. Then he died, right there in front of me." She choked back her sobs.

"I'm sorry, sweetheart, but what is so special about these glasses?" Billy asked.

"They're not just reading glasses. When you read a book while wearing them, that's when the magic starts. Somehow all the knowledge in the book is transferred to the reader.

"They also turn their wearer into a super-computer. The speed is incredible. I can read a four-hundred-page book in less than twenty minutes and completely understand every word and concept. In fact, the knowledge acquired from any book I read while wearing the glasses appears to stay forever in my memory. That's why they're called the book glasses."

"Where did Mr Harman get them?"

"I don't know. But they are over two-and-a-half centuries old and they were specially crafted for the pope at the time and for all future popes. I know this because the detectives who interviewed me immediately after Mr Harman's murder visited me again later to ask me about the glasses and they showed me what Mr Harman had on them. But how he got them is a mystery to me."

"The police asked you about the glasses?"

"Yes, I told them I didn't know anything about them and I'm sure they believed me. The police haven't got a clue I have them and I'm puzzled how the thugs knew about me and where to find me."

Billy could see the fear in Sam's eyes and was even more frightened for her. "Pope's glasses? Maybe someone from the Catholic church may know something about them?"

Her eyes were frantic. "No, Billy. The reason I'm still alive is that I don't ask questions. And you must never ask any questions or mention the glasses to anyone!"

"Sorry, I understand. Does anyone else know?"

"Yes, I told one other person after I was frightened due to the terrifying visions I started seeing. But don't worry, she wouldn't tell a soul, even if her life was threatened."

"Okay, what do you mean by 'terrifying visions' and who did you tell, sweetheart?"

"I discovered that if I wore the book glasses for more than eight hours at a time, I started to see visions of dead people. I told a friend at the local women's refuge, Sister Sue, who runs the place, who gave me a better understanding of what was happening. I now know not to wear them longer than eight hours at a time."

Billy held her again, trying to understand what all this meant. What were these glasses? Why did they have this power?

But they weren't the most pressing questions. The most important thing in all this was how the thugs had found out about Sam and what did they do about it?

PAYING OFF THE LOAN SHARK

Nothing else was said about the book glasses that afternoon as they continued to unpack Sam's belongings. By the time Billy returned the rented trailer and got back, Sam was dressed and ready to go out to dinner.

They dined at the same Chinese restaurant as on their previous visit but this time they chose the buffet and avoided any alcohol. They both need their wits about them. They planned to start small to avoid attracting any attention.

"Let's set our cut off at fifty thousand dollars," Sam said.

"Why fifty thousand?"

"If we win any more than that per day, it will set off alarm bells at the casino and two things could happen. One, we could be interrogated or two, asked to leave."

"How do you—"

"Please don't ask how I know all this. Just trust me that I know."

Billy nodded.

"So, given a maximum of fifty thousand per day, hopefully, in three days we can win all the money we need. That's the plan and two idiots with a plan will always do better than the smartest people in the world without one." She smiled. "Are you on board with that, Billy?"

He saluted. "Yes, ma'am."

"I like the way that sounded." Sam kissed him passionately.

They set off for the foyer of the casino, where Sam approached one of the staff. "Hello, I would like to speak to Frederick Hans, the VIP Casino Manager, please."

"Yes, ma'am. Your name, please?" the attendant asked as she picked up her phone.

"Samantha Page."

After a short pause, the attendant said, "Thank you, Samantha. Would you care to take a seat in our VIP lounge? Mr Hans will be down to see you in a few minutes. In the meantime, please help yourself to a complimentary snack and beverage. I've unlocked the door to your left."

They walked into the VIP lounge, Billy's mouth dropping open, which brought a smile to Sam's face as she watched him explore everything on offer. Despite the two of them being alone in the room, the tables were filled with an assortment of hot and cold food and beverages. The opulent furniture and décor paled in comparison with the spectacular harbour view.

Billy couldn't stop grinning. "Do you know how long I've been coming here, Sam, and I had no idea any of this existed, it's magnificent." He picked her up and spun her around.

"Put me down. Don't get used to this, okay? And don't forget what we're here for!" Sam whispered in his ear.

He put her down and sat next to her and they looked out over the harbour as the attendant served them Cokes in long thin glasses filled with ice.

"Sorry to keep you waiting, Samantha. Great to see you again and welcome back," Frederick said with his usual flair, looking even more immaculate than last time, with a beautiful white rose in his lapel.

Samantha took his offered hand and shook it. "Hello, Frederick. This is my fiancé, Billy Ashley."

"Hello, may I call you Billy?" Frederick said and, without waiting for a reply, continued, "Welcome. How can I help you two beautiful people today? Are you here to take up my offer by any chance, Samantha?"

"Would ten thousand dollars be a good starting point?" Sam's voice commanded the room.

"Of course, my dear. This way, please, follow me. Leave your drinks here and Tony will deliver fresh ones to your table. Thank you, Tony."

He led them to a private elevator and ushered them inside. "The room we are going to is just three floors up. I will take you to the cashier where you can pick up your chips as soon as you transfer the money. Then pick a table and have fun. By the way, I just love your glasses, Samantha."

The doors opened and Frederick led them into a gaming room. "I will leave you here and the cashier will look after you. Please don't hesitate to call me at any time. I'm here all night, so enjoy. Tony will bring you your drinks as soon as you pick a table and good luck."

After thanking the cashier, Sam called out, "Billy, come hold the chips for me."

"Wow, Sam, this is incredible. We are really going to do this!" Billy was having trouble keeping still.

"You need to calm down and please let me do all the talking. You will pretend to be the main player with all the money, and you allow me to play because I bring you luck. Get it?" Sam whispered in his ear and kissed him.

He looked confused. "Okay, why didn't you tell me this before?"

"Are we going to do this or what?" Sam said impatiently.

"Sorry, yes, I get it now."

"Just play along with me, okay? Remember, don't gamble, just keep me playing poker first and then blackjack. Let's do this!"

At the poker table, their chips started piling up and the onlookers all seemed to fall for their act hook, line, and sinker. Sam knew that if these people believed them, then the casino surveillance team observing their every move through strategically placed hidden cameras, would fall for it as well and leave them alone.

Three hours later, after playing poker and then blackjack, they had accumulated thirty thousand dollars in winnings and Sam called for the attendant to hold their chips. Ensuring Billy wasn't left behind to gamble it all away, she took him by the arm and headed to the VIP lounge for a much-needed break.

"I'm going to the bathroom. Can you please wait for me here? You've been wonderful all night so let's not fuck things up now, okay?" Sam said. When he didn't respond, she almost shouted, "Are you listening to me, Billy?"

But Billy's attention was on a flat-screen TV on the wall. "Look, Sam. Isn't that where you used to work? There's been a murder at the museum. Did you know her?"

"What?" Sam turned towards the TV. "Oh my God, they've murdered Dr Julie Dunn!"

After hearing the details of the murder on the news bulletin, Sam ran to the bathroom, broke down and cried.

She had a chilling thought. She knew how the three thugs had discovered her name and come to find her at her old apartment. They must have tortured Dr Dunn before killing her. But she reminded herself that the book glasses had been given to her and it wasn't her fault that both Mr Harman and Dr Dunn were dead.

She splashed water on her face and quickly fixed up her make up before heading back out into the lounge.

"Sorry about your friend, sweetheart. Are you okay?" Billy wrapped his arms around her and held her tightly.

"Thanks, honey. I'm fine now. Let's get back in and finish this off."

"Hey, I may not be a good gambler, but I'll make an excellent partner, if you'll let me. Will you let me, Sam?"

"Yes, of course, honey."

"Okay, as your partner, I'm telling you we are not going back in there after this horrible news. We're going home. Please don't argue with me about this. Tell Frederick to hold our winnings and we'll be back tomorrow. Off you go!"

"You're right. I love you!" Sam said with relief.

All the way home to Billy's apartment, Sam kept on thinking about how Julie must have suffered before they killed her like they'd killed Mr Harman. She didn't care now if they found her. She couldn't wait to deal with them when the time came.

She wasn't that scared person anymore—a fire ignited within her and her thoughts turned to revenge. But it would not be blind revenge. It would be calculated, masterfully set out, so by the time they finally got to her, they wouldn't know what had hit them.

She knew exactly what to do and silently swore to see her plan through until all three murderers were dealt with once and for all.

"Are you okay, sweetheart? Do you feel like talking?" Billy asked gently as she continued to gaze out of the ferry's window into the darkness.

"Sorry?" Sam asked. "Oh, by the way, tomorrow is Monday and it's a public holiday, so I don't have uni."

"Yes, I know. I'm off work tomorrow too."

"On public holidays, the casino always has a bigger crowd than on weekends, which are traditionally busiest. I think tomorrow would be a great opportunity for us to get the remaining hundred and twenty thousand dollars. But if we do it, it will be almost impossible for us to get back to the casino again. Although they may not know how we won, consistent winnings of that magnitude will raise suspicion and they are likely to simply ban us for life.

"But if we do it all tomorrow, we may be lucky enough to avoid the worst-case scenario, because there are likely be others like us, and casino surveillance and security might be too busy putting out other fires to notice us."

He looked dazed but didn't argue. "Whatever you think."

PLEASE CALL FREDERICK HANS

"Wake up, sleepyhead. It's Monday!" Sam yelled from the kitchen.

"Come back to bed," Billy pleaded, half-asleep.

"While you've been asleep, I've already been to the supermarket for some groceries and picked up some breakfast, so come and eat it before it gets cold. Oh, and by the way, I think I saw those three thugs," Sam said casually.

"What!" Billy screamed and tore into the kitchen wearing only boxer shorts.

"Yes, those three thugs who were looking for me at my old apartment. Was one of them shorter and bulkier than the other two with short grey hair and a beard?" Sam asked, before biting into her egg and bacon muffin.

"Yes, that's right, and the other two were taller and thinner and both were balding," Billy looked through the front window, frantic.

"What are you doing, silly? We're two floors up and you can't see the street from here. I don't think they would be lying on the beach so come and have your breakfast." Sam sipped on her cappuccino.

"They've found us. How could you eat at a time like this?" Billy ran back to the front window for another look outside.

"Billy, come here, please!" Sam said.

He stormed back into the kitchen.

"Thank you. Now listen. They might live here, who knows? Now that we've seen them, we can avoid them. Before they could have been in right in front of us and we wouldn't have had a clue. So, stop worrying for nothing. They haven't found shit. Now eat your breakfast before it gets cold." Sam settled him down and smiled when she saw him tuck in.

She needed Billy calm so she could think things through. She'd had a headache all night and didn't want to wear the book glasses until they arrived at the casino, expecting another long night with them on.

She took two headache pills with breakfast and went to lie down after putting the groceries away and cleaning up the kitchen.

Still spooked, Billy stayed in the apartment all day, occasionally sneaking a peek out of the front windows when he thought Sam wasn't looking.

Before they knew it, the sun was setting, and it was time to head out to the casino. They dressed with the high roller room in mind. Sam suggested Billy wear his so-called funeral suit, and she donned a magnificent long black dress with an open laced back, with matching shoes and handbag.

On such a beautiful moonlit night, the ferry ride should have been romantic, but they had no time for romance, with Sam whispering instructions in Billy's ear all the way. By the time they docked, she was confident he wouldn't let her down and excited to again enter the domain of the high rollers.

After putting on the book glasses, Samantha approached

the front desk in the main foyer of the casino. "Hello, could you please call Frederick Hans for me?" Billy stood next to her with a half-smile.

"Welcome. My name is Ted. May I ask your name, please?" the attendant said with a smile.

"Samantha Page and Billy Ashley."

"Thank you." He reached for the phone.

Ted had just hung up the phone when a young woman appeared at his side. "Welcome back, Samantha and Billy, we have been expecting you. My name is Pam Wong. Unfortunately, Mr Hans is currently unavailable, but I will be happy to assist you any way I can. Whenever you are ready, please make your way to the third floor. The cashier is expecting you." She led them to the lift and pressed the up button. "I will leave you here but if you need anything, please ask for me and I will be happy to assist you."

Once the lift doors closed, Sam whispered to Billy, "See, what did I tell you? It's so busy here tonight that Frederick couldn't see us because his hands are full taking care of his wealthier clients. Let's do this!"

When they arrived on the third floor, they joined the end of the cashier line. The room was buzzing with activity and excitement.

After a short wait, the cashier arranged an attendant to take their winnings over to their chosen table. Sam started with blackjack and quickly began to accumulate significant winnings, yet no one raised an eyebrow at them.

As Sam had predicted, the high roller room was packed and huge quantities of money were being wagered, won, and lost at tables all around the room.

Four hours in, with eighty-four thousand dollars in winnings, Sam's headache had become unbearable. She raised her hand to decline to bet on a new round of cards and called for a bathroom break. The other players ignored her.

In crippling pain, Sam took off the book glasses and handed them to Billy and told him to take her seat while she took a short break.

Billy sat down and ogled the pair of glasses in his hand.

"Sir, are you playing? Excuse me, sir, you must play if you are sitting at the table," the dealer said.

"Sorry, are you talking to me?" Billy asked.

"Sir, you must play if you continue to sit at the table. Are you playing, sir?"

"Um, yes, I'm playing," Billy replied and slipped on the book glasses.

After putting them on, he was overwhelmed by a strange sensation, almost as if a strong wind was blowing his hair back. Suddenly self-conscious and fearing he would be exposed, he opened his eyes and nervously studied the dealer and the other players, but no one gave him a second glance.

"Do you wish to place a bet, sir?" the dealer asked, directing his attention back to the game.

He nodded, awestruck at what was happening in his mind. At first, he was alarmed by his sudden ability to see the cards of all the players, no matter where they were placed on the table. He also absorbed all sorts of information, everything from a slight movement made by someone to a hitch in breathing or a raised heart rate.

All the while, the complex calculations his mind were computing were breathtaking. The adrenaline hit was potent and addictive.

Buoyed by a surge of newfound confidence, he placed an

initial bet of five thousand dollars. He didn't know how he got to that figure as his previous highest initial bet was one hundred dollars, but surprisingly, it didn't faze him. He confidently raised the stakes until his winnings were tenfold.

Uncharacteristic of him, he showed no sign of emotion and switched into an automatic mode of playing, knowing what to do and how to do it.

Almost three hours later, with winnings exceeding one hundred and forty-six thousand dollars, Billy realised Sam still wasn't back and quickly took off the book glasses and placed them in the inside pocket of his suit jacket.

He informed the dealer he wished to cash in his chips. An attendant appeared to accompany him to the cashier, and he asked him to hold his winnings while he visited the bathroom and rushed off to the VIP lounge to find Sam.

"Billy, I'm over here!" Sam called out as she sipped on a glass of champagne while eating a cucumber sandwich. "You must try these sandwiches. The cream cheese spread in-between the cucumber slices is to die for."

"Sam, you frightened the shit out of me. Where have you been? Have you been here the entire time?" Billy whispered in her ear.

"No need to whisper among this lot and it took you long enough to come looking for me. Anyway, how did you go with it all?" Sam asked, reaching for another sandwich.

"We won!" Billy said.

"Of course we won, silly! How did you go with wearing the book glasses?" Sam put down her sandwich.

"What a rush. What can I say?"

"I know!" she said with a smile and settled back down on the lounge to finish off the remaining sandwiches and wash them down with the last of her champagne. "Come on, let's collect our winnings and go. So how much have we won?"

"A little over one hundred and forty-six thousand dollars," Billy said without much thought. Then, astonished by the amount, he started to hyperventilate.

"Take it easy, Billy, breathe in and out. Take deep breaths. You're still coming down from the rush of the book glasses. You are perfectly fine, okay? This will pass in a few minutes. Just keep breathing like that. See? There you go. Now how do you feel?" Sam asked rubbing his back.

"Yes, much better thanks. My mind is still racing with endless ideas and calculations. It's amazing!" Billy explained breathing heavily.

"Okay, I need some fresh air, so you go back and cash in the chips and I'll meet you out the front of the casino."

Billy rushed off to the cashier. When he walked out the main entrance of the casino, he was terrified to see Sam flat on her back in the middle of the driveway with a crowd gathered around her.

He ran over to her and was relieved to see her being helped back onto her feet by a couple of bystanders. She brushed it off as simply tripping and falling, but he knew there was something more to it as he held her tightly while thanking the crowd for their help.

"What happened, sweetheart?" he asked as he helped her walk to the wharf to catch the ferry home.

"Did you get the money?" Sam asked.

"Yes, I've got it here." He showed her the cheque and put it safely back in his wallet.

"Good. I'm fine. I now know that alcohol and the book glasses don't go together. Lesson learnt and never to be repeated!" Sam said, slurring her words.

Although taking a little longer than usual to get back to the apartment, they made it home without any further drama and, exhausted, slept off the magnificent achievement without any celebration or acknowledgement.

Nothing was said about it again; the fear was too great for them to ever talk about it. They knew it was a miracle that they had not attracted attention from casino security despite their winning streak and the fact they both wore the same glasses at the poker and blackjack tables.

The next morning Billy decided to take the day off work. Careful to avoid waking up Sam, he picked up his surfboard and hit the waves. By the time he got back to the apartment, she was up and eating her breakfast.

The rest of the morning was filled with organising how he would go about paying off the loan shark. "I'm still four thousand dollars short," Billy said.

"Don't worry. I'll transfer that to you now on my mobile."

"Thanks, sweet—"

"You just make sure this never happens again!"

Billy didn't say a word. He just nodded vigorously. He didn't want to experience that kind of pressure ever again.

"Okay, it's done," she said, winding her arms around him. "Now, university needs to be my priority for a while. I've got exams coming up. You need to support me by not going back to your old ways."

He shook his head. "I swear I won't. I don't want to let you down."

"Good." She smiled and kissed him.

HIGH DISTINCTIONS

Relieved, she renewed her focus on her studies, setting a plan in motion to double her workload over the next two semesters. If she was successful in attaining high distinctions for all eight first-year subjects over this period, she could present a good argument to fast-track her degree. Her goal was to slash two years off a three-year full-time bachelor's degree.

She had ditched the idea of a double degree to focus only on her Bachelor of Law for the sole purpose of getting into a PhD course as soon as possible. The PhD research degree she'd already decided on would give her the highest education which should carry her through life's most difficult challenges. Plus, it would give her the stability she'd always wanted—she would never be out of work again.

But she had to make it happen before she was discovered, and the book glasses were taken away from her forever.

She began hitting the books every chance she got, careful to restrict wearing the glasses to a maximum of eight hours at a time and scheduling long breaks to avoid suffering the horrendous side effects.

But there was also the worry of the men who had attacked Billy. What if they tried something again? What if they came for them both? There was no doubt in her mind that they'd been after the glasses. She went to the library and borrowed Bruce Lee's *Chinese Gung Fu: The Philosophical Art of Self-Defense* for some light reading.

But while the book glasses could help train her mind, she knew she needed to train her body as well. She hunted online for the best self-defence classes available and made bookings with a few to see which would best suit her needs.

Billy was curious when he realised what she'd done. "Self-defence classes? Really? On top of all your studying?"

She shrugged. "Sure. Why don't you do it too? It's a great way to keep fit."

But she saw realisation on his face, and he took her in his arms. "Darling, is this because of those men? Are you worried they'll come back?"

She didn't want to worry him so tried not to look too concerned. "A little. I just thought it was worth it, you know?"

He flexed his arms. "Yeah, maybe you're right. But I don't think I want to do it too. I can pack a decent punch already."

———

Days turned into weeks and weeks into months. Before she knew it, she had achieved high distinctions for each of her eight subjects. In light of this outstanding result, she was confident she could make an argument to get her credits on the grounds of prior learning, so the university could waive the remaining sixteen subjects and award her a Bachelor of Law Degree, which would allow her to move straight on to a PhD course.

Sam waited after knocking on Professor Grasim's door.

"Come in."

She opened the door. "Hello, Professor. It's Sam Page. Can I see you, please? Do you have time?"

"Come in, Samantha," the professor said with a smile. "I know what you are here for. First, congratulations on achieving an incredible eight high distinctions. We ask for it every year but when we finally get it, we are truly astonished at the remarkable accomplishment. Well done. Well done indeed."

"Thank you, Professor. Have you had a chance to read my email yet?"

"Yes, and I don't think there will be any problem. I just need to run it by the faculty board, and I will get back to you soon. No one is likely to object, and I will be thrilled to see you moving into a PhD research course. I don't need to tell you about the difference between course work and completing a thesis. I'm sure you know the significance of doing an original body of research."

"Yes, and thank you again, Professor," Sam said as she reached out her hand to shake his.

"No, thank you for your hard work. We are all proud of you at the faculty."

As she walked back to her studio apartment, she thought back over the previous several months and couldn't believe how fast the time had flown. Billy had been wonderful and patient with her and she'd managed to schedule her wearing of the book glasses in such a way to avoid the nightmarish visions and inflicting serious injury on herself.

Also, miraculously, she had not yet been discovered by the three thugs who were looking for her.

When her thoughts turned to Dr Julie Dunn, she was saddened by her unnecessary death and, at the same time, her blood boiled. But she always pushed those feelings aside. It was not yet time for revenge. She needed to focus on her education and was determined to see it through.

Once inside her apartment, Sam put on the book glasses to check her email and was pleased to find her presence had been requested back in the professor's office at 9 a.m. the next day. She knew the decision had been made and she would be informed of the outcome. Confident it would go her way, she hit the books even harder and continued studying late into the night.

The next morning, Sam headed off to the law faculty building for her 9 a.m. meeting.

"Come in, please," said the professor in response to her knock and Sam opened the door without any hesitation. "Samantha, good morning."

"Thank you for this meeting," Sam said, shocked to see the entire law faculty teaching staff gathered in Professor Grasim's office.

"Samantha, please come and stand over here next to me," the professor said with a welcoming wave. She joined him. "Once in a while, a student comes along who is exceptional. Their discipline and work ethic are so unmatched that they achieve great heights.

"With a result of eight out of eight high distinctions for your Bachelor's degree, we believe you are that exceptional student. Therefore, in response to your request and after much deliberation, the faculty has granted you the sixteen credits needed to complete your degree and acceptance into a research degree as a PhD candidate starting next semester. On behalf of the law faculty, congratulations and well done!"

There was an outbreak of applause.

"Thank you, Professor. Thank you to the whole faculty. I will not let you down," Sam said, tears streaming down her face.

A couple of staff members brought in an assortment of hot and cold drinks and plates of gourmet sandwiches, mini quiches, tarts, and tiny cupcakes. Starstruck, over the next two hours, Sam mingled with the staff. The offers of support she received were remarkable, but the show of how impressed these academics, authorities in their field, were with her was even more remarkable.

How did I get here? She was proud of how far she'd come but knew that without the book glasses she would not be there.

The two-hour experience was something she never forgot and, upon leaving, she found a quiet place in the grounds of the university to call Billy and tell him all about it.

"Billy, Billy, I got credits for my remaining subjects and was also accepted into a Doctorate for next semester and Professor Grasim announced it in front of the entire law faculty staff. Can you believe it?" Sam poured her heart out over the phone, and they continued talking for over twenty minutes.

"I'm happy for you, sweetheart, but I need to go back to work now. How about you come to my place for dinner tonight and we can celebrate then?"

"I'd love to! See you tonight!" said Sam and she wandered back to her room, still walking on a cloud, trying to forget that she owed everything to the book glasses.

DOCTOR OF PHILOSOPHY LAW

March 2015

"Welcome to all Doctor of Philosophy Law candidates. It's a new semester with some new faces, so congratulations to all of you for being accepted into our program. I warn you, it's a very demanding one.

"I'm Professor Alexander Grasim, Head of the Law Faculty. You may research one of the following research themes on the screen behind me. Please take a few minutes to look them over."

Professor Grasim pointed at the screen on which the following text was displayed:

Research themes:

- Asian and Islamic law
- Children, youth, and families
- Citizenship, migration, and refugees
- Commercial and international commercial law
- Constitutional and administrative law

- Corporate, securities and finance law
- Criminal law, justice, and criminology
- Environmental law and climate change
- Health law, governance, and ethics
- Human rights and development
- Intellectual property, media, and privacy law
- International law
- Justice, legal process, and the profession
- Jurisprudence and legal theory
- Labour, employment, and anti-discrimination law
- Legal history
- Private law: tort, contracts, equity, and property
- Taxation

The noise in the room increased as the students talked among themselves.

"Settle down, please! Thank you. By now, you have all selected your supervisor or have been appointed a supervisor. Please meet with them by the end of the week before you get your teaching schedule. These timetables are not negotiable; accept them and move on.

"Teaching responsibilities are equally important to your research, so suck it up and work around them. No allowances will be made, especially for those creative PhD candidates who come up with the most ridiculous excuses. I have heard it all, people, and will not tolerate it. You have been informed."

Some laughter could be heard around the room, but Professor Grasim continued. "Some of you full-timers will most likely complete your coursework and produce a successful thesis and graduate in less than the allocated three to four years. For the part-timers, we have timeframes for you so please check them and clarify them with your supervisor. Familiarise yourselves with your timeframes and deadlines and work closely with your supervisor to ensure that you remain on track.

"If you have any questions, please see your supervisor. Don't come to me. I will not see PhD candidates unless I ask for you, so please don't forget that. Also, I will meet regularly with your supervisors, so if your heart is not in it or you have reservations, then I will know about it. If that is the case, you don't want a summons to my office. I have no problem with people changing their minds as a result of the pressure, family, or work commitments; I respect that.

"My priority has and will always be to do everything in my power, through your supervisors, to help you all get over the line if you have the desire and the drive to do so. That's my promise. All you need to do is please notify your supervisor before it's too late. If you can do that, then you have my full support. Good luck, thank you!"

Professor Grasim packed up his gear and headed for the door. Sam knew she had to catch him before he left. She hadn't been given a supervisor and knew how crucial it was to get the right person. She'd assumed someone would be assigned to her. That's what she thought the professor's letter had suggested, anyway.

"Excuse me, Professor, about my supervisor, sir!" Sam called over the crowd to him as he walked past her on his way out of the lecture theatre.

"Sorry, I can't talk now. I'm in a hurry. Come see me in my office in ten minutes," he yelled back.

Precisely ten minutes later, Sam knocked on the professor's door.

"Come in, please."

"Thank you, Professor," Sam replied nervously.

"How can I help you, Samantha?" Professor Grasim asked.

"I must be the only one without a supervisor. I don't know

what to do," Sam said, her anxiety making her voice shake. This whole thing was stressful enough without this on top of it.

"Why didn't you say that I instructed you in my official letter not to bother getting a supervisor?" he asked with a grin.

That's what she'd thought it said but she'd assumed he must have misworded it. "I'm confused."

"I'll make it easy for you, I would like to be your supervisor."

"But you just said..." Sam was lost for words.

"I know what I said, but you are exceptional, and I don't want anyone else to share in the glory of your achievements."

"You mean, you are taking a risk on me and no one else wants the responsibility?"

He seemed surprised at her perception and laughed but did not confirm or deny her statement. Then, with a burst of excitement, he said, "I must tell you, your methodology presentation last week left my entire law faculty teaching staff speechless. These people are the best in their field of research, so it was priceless to see someone knocking their socks off.

"Your topic of 'Copyright Protection Laws in the Age of Data Sharing: legal challenges and responses in the context of online behavioural marketing' was special. You left them with nowhere to go. You covered it all, and your methodology about regulatory models characterised by individual consent and the necessity of testing was most valuable and left them all with their mouths open.

"Did you notice they all walked out of the room in total silence? That has never happened before! Thank you for giving me that experience, Samantha. I will always cherish it."

She felt her body relax. "Really? I was concerned I may have missed the mark."

"No, quite the opposite. You intimidated them all."

"Thank you, Professor, but that was not my intention."

"Yes, and that's the best part because they knew that."

"I don't know what to say," Sam said bashfully.

"Well, I'm your supervisor and that's that. Over the next month, I would like you to work out a timeframe for our regular meetings and a possible halfway mark for completing your thesis. Remember, you have three to four years to complete it."

"I've already done that and more."

"What do you mean?" he asked, looking confused.

"I mean, I have done all that and have estimated my completion date, taking in account all my data modelling testing outcomes," Sam replied.

He held up his hands. "Okay, hold onto that for now. Email me the details and we can discuss it when we first meet. But I am curious, when do you see yourself completing your thesis?"

"Well, in half the time you specified."

"Half of four years?"

"No, half of three years!"

"I'm sorry I asked. Never mind that now. Look, I'll see you in a month and we can talk about it then. I have work for you to do and I'm sure you also have a life." He stood and stretched out his hand.

"Thank you, Professor, for being my supervisor." Sam rose and shook his hand firmly.

"It's my honour, Samantha. I'm sure you will do me proud."

Once outside the law faculty building, she rang Billy to tell him the wonderful news and arranged to meet him at their favourite Italian restaurant, near his place, at 7 p.m. All the way back to her studio apartment, her feet barely touched the ground. She was so excited that everything was going to plan.

Leftover quiche made for a quick lunch before she headed over to the refuge. It had been over a year since she'd visited, and she felt guilty about not keeping in touch with Sister Sue and not even leaving her a contact number.

The strain of cutting Sister Sue out of her life after everything she'd done had caught up with her and she didn't know how to make it up to her. Knowing that the sister didn't like accepting gifts, Sam hoped she would accept her invitation to have dinner with Billy and her.

DINNER INVITATION

"Come in, please," Samantha heard Sister Sue say after gently knocking at her office door.

She went in. "Hello, Sister Sue. Before you kick me out, I would like to apologise for my appalling behaviour," Sam said with a shaky voice, glad to see her friend and mentor once again after all this time.

The sister looked shocked but pleased. "Samantha, darling, please come in. I would never kick you out of my office, dear. As long as I'm here, you are always welcome. Please sit down."

She came around her desk and stood in front of Sam. "Look at you, you are so beautiful, my darling. Never mind about apologising, I was much to blame. Now, sit down and tell me what you have been doing. I've missed you so much, especially our daily discussions on everyday things happening at the refuge that you haven't had a chance to find out about since you've been gone." Sister Sue hesitated for a moment before going back to sit at her desk.

"Thank you. I have the entire afternoon free for you, if you haven't anything planned, that is?" Sam said and walked over to give her a huge hug and a kiss on her cheek.

Sister Sue held her close. "Oh, wonderful. I would love that. How about we catch up over tea with jam and scones like we used to?"

"On one condition."

"Oh, what's that?"

"That you come to dinner tonight with Billy and me."

"Who's Billy?"

"Billy is my boyfriend, and you can meet him tonight if you come to dinner," she said with a huge smile.

"How can I say no to such an invitation? I would love to join you for dinner and meet your Billy. How long have you been dating?"

"Let's go have some tea and scones and I'll tell you all about it." Sam grabbed her arm and headed for the door.

They caught up on all they had missed out on in each other's lives since that difficult day. They also laughed and cried, reflecting on both the good times and the bad that they'd experienced in the years since Sam had moved to Sydney.

Sam felt guilty about not keeping in touch with her. She had missed Sue's company, and Sue seemed overjoyed to see her, so she decided not to let that happen again.

Nearly four hours later, Sam left to go home and change and told Sister Sue she would be back at six to pick her up for dinner. To avoid the gauntlet of well-wishers from the refuge's regulars, who would ask where she'd been and talk about how she'd changed, Sam arranged to meet her around the corner from the refuge.

———

Billy was waiting when Sam unlocked the front door and walked into his apartment with Sister Sue close behind. "Here we are, Sister Sue, this is Billy. Billy, I would like you to meet Sister Sue."

"Finally, I'm meeting the famous Sister Sue! I have heard so much about you. Please come in and welcome to our apartment." Billy gave her a warm handshake and took Sam's hand in his.

"Thank you, Billy. Very nice to meet you." She gave a smile of approval.

"Great timing, ladies; it's 7 p.m. The restaurant is just around the corner so let's make our way there. What do you say?"

"Lead the way. We're right behind you, honey." Sam interlocked her arm with the sister and followed Billy out.

———

Right from the beginning, Sue was impressed with Billy and by the time they ordered dessert, she understood why Sam was in love with him. She was in awe of how they finished each other sentences, touched each other gently and the way they would fondly glance at one another. It reminded her of the days she'd had with Sam's father before that fatal day when her life had changed forever.

She found herself desperately yearning to tell Sam all about it and mustered all her strength to contain herself before she exploded with the emotions she'd kept in check for far too long.

"Excuse me, Sister Sue, I know it's late, but I was hoping you might have time to come back to the apartment for a cup of tea or coffee. We would love your company. How about it? I promise we won't take too much of your time," Billy asked.

"Yes, of course. Thank you for asking. By the way, earlier you said, 'our apartment', so did you mean it's Sam's and yours?" She looked at Sam.

"It sure is, sister. I put the apartment in both our names after Sam helped me with the deposit. But technically, it's the bank's until I pay off the mortgage." Billy laughed. "Did she tell you she'll also be teaching university students while she's completing her research degree? Can you believe that?"

Sam had mentioned it, although avoiding her eyes as she did so. Sue plastered a smile on her face. "Yes Billy, she told me, and I'm just as impressed as you are."

Sue wasn't happy that Sam not only still had the book glasses but was actively using them. She knew that something so precious had a dark side to it and hoped beyond everything that her daughter wouldn't be drawn irretrievably into its web.

TEACHING UNDERGRADS

After tea and coffee at their place, Sister Sue gratefully accepted their kind offer to walk her back to Manly Wharf and see her off. With Billy sandwiched in between the two women, they headed out and started talking about the wonderful night they had just enjoyed.

Billy looked at the sister thoughtfully. "Sorry to interrupt you ladies, but something has been bothering me all night and I need to ask you about it."

"What, Billy? Don't keep us waiting," Sam said, annoyed at his interruption.

"Are you sure you two are not related?" Billy carefully scrutinised them both.

"What are you talking about, silly? Do we look related?" Sam replied with her hands on her hips.

"Well, yes, you do, actually. I noticed the first moment I saw you together when you arrived at the apartment and dismissed it, thinking it was my imagination. But during dinner at the restaurant, I noticed your hand and face actions are similar.

"Wait, hear me out. Yes, you look a little different, but that's because of the age difference. Just look at your hands for goodness' sake."

Billy stopped talking as she and Sister Sue frowned at him. "Sorry, Sister Sue, I don't know what has gotten into him. Billy, stop embarrassing me."

"Sam, can't you see it?" Billy asked.

It was rare she got angry with Billy, but this was her reunion with Sister Sue. Why was he behaving this way? "Billy, you're ruining the night." She was mortified by the shocked look on the sister's face.

"I'm sorry, Sam," he said. "It's probably just my imagination." He tentatively took her hand. "I love Sam so much I think I see a bit of her in everyone."

By the time they got to the wharf, everyone had recovered, and they ended the night just the way Sam had hoped they would, with a commitment to see each other regularly.

A few weeks later, Sam received a text from Sister Sue about organising their next dinner date. Thrilled to hear from her so soon, she immediately called Billy, momentarily forgetting she was in the midst of a half-day meeting with the professor, who suddenly walked back into the room, quickly ending her conversation.

"Thank you for agreeing to my schedule and timeframes, but this teaching responsibility is a bit early for me, don't you think, Professor?" she asked.

"Hang on, I said your schedule and timeframes are a good start, so let's leave it at that. As far as your teaching responsibilities, whatever do you mean?"

"I can't do public speaking," Sam blurted out.

He scowled. "I have no times for games. I know what you are trying to do, and you are not getting out of teaching just so you can focus on your research. I'm not having that, okay?

You're teaching tomorrow and that's it. You have been emailed all your presentations, you know the subject material, get on with it. You have two undergrad classes per week and make sure you meet the head lecturer before you start your first class."

"I'm teaching undergrads!" Sam said, thinking out loud as she picked up her things and headed out the door.

———

The next day, after a short meeting with the head lecturer of the School of Law, she found herself hurrying to her first teaching class. After promising to never be late for them, she conceded she was about to break that promise on her first day.

She stopped short at the door of the lecture theatre to catch her breath and adjust the book glasses before walking in. With new-found confidence, she entered the theatre, amazed to see close to three hundred undergrads waiting for the class to start. She was livid that no one had warned her about the ridiculous numbers.

"Hey, stupid, you better sit down before the professor walks in," someone in the front row called out, drawing the attention of all the students in the lecture theatre.

Ignoring him, she walked up to the lectern and deposited her notes on top. "My name is Samantha Page and welcome to Business Law. This undergraduate subject has an emphasis on the wide range of career options open to graduates who combine specialist knowledge of business law with studies in business, accounting, marketing, economics, finance, or government.

"Career opportunities include accountant, financial analyst, investment adviser, policy advisor, compliance and regulatory specialist, tax adviser, financial broker and financial planner. Do I have your attention now?" She gave her audience a huge smile.

Yes, she did have their full attention. She enjoyed their shocked reactions that someone so young would be their teacher. Even those high up the back row, where faces were hard to distinguish, were silent.

As they all sat there all with their mouths agape, the same individual in the front row who had yelled at her put his hand up and waited patiently for Sam to notice him.

"Yes, you with your hand up." She realised that he was not much older than her.

"Sorry for my outburst, Professor, you look so young and I thought you were a student," he called out, to the horror of the rest of the students.

"What's your name?" Sam asked.

"Luke. Sorry, I mean Luke Anderson," he replied nervously.

"Well, Luke Anderson, guess what? I'm not a professor. I am a PhD student here. So, there's no need to apologise."

"If you're not a professor, how is it that you are teaching?" Luke asked on behalf of everyone else in the room.

"There is a mandatory teaching component in the PhD postgraduate research degree in which I am enrolled. So, I'm afraid to say, you'll need to put up with me for the entire semester."

In no time at all she was in full flight, flicking through the slides and answering questions on the subject matter which she knew like the back of her hand.

Ten minutes into the two-hour lesson, she noticed a student stand up and walk out, closely followed by another two students. Sam's heart started to beat faster as she tried to understand why they were leaving, when she noticed another two students get up and leave.

Focusing on her lesson became more difficult as students began to exit the room by the dozen.

Realising that she had control of the class, Sam stopped the lesson and gave the class five minutes to complete an exercise that wasn't scheduled to be done until the second lesson so she could investigate.

Sam rushed out the door to catch the last two students exiting the theatre. "Excuse me, why is everyone leaving my class?"

"This class is available online, so we don't need to be here in person," one of them said.

Her friend added, "Also, we have four weeks to lock in a subject and most of us use this time to try out a few different subjects to see if they suit us."

"And it's adult learning so we can come and go any time we like, but everyone goes to the first class to check out the professor."

"Yes, of course. Thank you for that."

"That's okay, Professor. See you." They both waved and continued on their way.

Their explanations took a load off Sam's shoulders and she was able to resume the lesson when she returned. If she hadn't been so caught up with the overall fear of teaching, she would have recalled her experience and not bothered worrying about what students thought of her or why they were leaving her class.

By the end of the lesson, she was more fearless than she could ever have imagined which allowed her to focus on the task at hand and not sweat the small stuff.

DR SAMANTHA PAGE

August 2017

"Come in," Sam called after finishing a call with Billy.

"Excuse me, are you Dr Samantha Page?" A sweet voice asked. A young woman took a hesitant step into her office.

"Yes, I am. How can I help you?" Sam said from her desk.

"I'm a new student and my friends told me to come and see you about transferring into your business law class," she asked, taking another step.

"What's your name, please?"

"My name is Wee Ying."

"Wee Ying, your friends gave you incorrect advice. You will need to go to the administration building, right next door to this building, to request a transfer. I cannot help you with that. Do you understand?"

"I understand, thank you," Ying replied, smiling.

"Good. It's the same place where you first enrolled in your classes, remember?" Sam said with a wave as she watched her walk out.

Just as she resumed marking the paper in front of her, she heard another knock on her office door. "I told you, it's the building next door!" She called without looking up as she kept on marking.

"You said no such thing. What about the building next door?" Professor Grasim asked as he took a seat.

"Sorry, Professor. I thought you were a student!" Sam said, standing immediately.

"Sit down, sit down. Look, we need to talk about continuing your work here. What do you say?"

"What? Me, continuing to work here?"

"Yes, on a more permanent basis. What do you think?" he said with a grin.

"No way! I told you not to even think about it!"

"Okay, take it easy. It was just an idea." He waved his hands to try to calm her down.

"Just an idea! When you first brought it up, I told you no. Remember, when I accepted this teaching position six months ago just after I received my PhD, you said it would only be for six months. Well, next week those six months are up. It's just an idea? give me a break!" Sam said, annoyed he would try this again.

"Come on, Sam. I gave you a chance, remember? I'm only asking."

"Please don't do this to me. I understand and that's why I accepted this six-month position in the first place. But I've just got into my new apartment in the city and I need a job that will cover my living expenses. Sorry, but I'm finishing up next week as agreed."

"All I can say is that I gave it a good go. You can't blame me for trying." He winked.

"It's not funny. You know how much you and the faculty means to me." She was mad at him for pushing her buttons.

"Yes, I know, and we are all very proud of you, Dr Page, and would like to thank you for your professionalism and undying commitment over the last few years towards your research, colleagues and students. I will miss you dearly. After all, who am I going to needle when you are gone?" The professor finished off with a joke, but she could have sworn he was blinking tears out of his eyes.

———

By the time she'd left her teaching position at the university, Sam had secured a full-time job at the most prominent law firm in Sydney.

Stanley, Wise and Associates was fast becoming the most successful law firm in the country after a series of lawsuit wins regarding big business takeovers and company mergers over the past five years. They were renowned for their savvy and cutting-edge concepts and would often leave their opponents astounded by their lawful unorthodox approaches.

Sam secured a twelve-month contract for an undisclosed amount, rumoured around the law faculty to be in the millions, with a performance bonus attached to it, of course.

Although pleased with herself, the faculty was unaware she was far from satisfied with this achievement, but it was a step closer to her goal of one day starting her own business law firm.

Confident she already possessed the knowledge, aptitude, and technique to make it happen, all she desired from this position at Stanley, Wise and Associates was the experience and the contacts required to fulfil her dream and enable her to take the next step in her life.

As Sam walked to her new job with the sun on her face, she did so without a care in the world. Walking straight through to the high-end business part of the city, a place she'd once considered a no-go zone, she felt comfortable in her navy-blue pinstripe power suit with matching shoes and handbag.

Her destination was easy to find because it was the newest and highest structure in the city. The ride to the twenty-first floor took no time in one of the ten new elevators with all the bells and whistles. It opened directly into the foyer of Stanley, Wise and Associates as the firm took up the entire floor.

She approached the reception desk and asked for the CEO, Barry Stanley, and the receptionist directed her to take a seat.

"Sam, you're early. Please come in," Barry said as he strode into the foyer, his greying temples catching in the light from the windows.

"Thanks, Barry. Good morning." Sam looked up and smiled at him, then followed him into his magnificent office.

"Yes, good morning! Coffee or tea?" Barry asked while walking back behind his desk.

"Tea, please. I would love a little lemon in it, if you have it," Sam asked, taking a seat in one of the chairs in front of his desk.

"Did you get that, Betty?" Barry asked over the intercom and waited for her confirmation. "Sam, welcome to Stanley, Wise and Associates."

Sam nodded. "Thank you."

"Now, sorry to get straight into things, but we have a problem. It involves a business merger of enormous proportions, and I mean a monster, which has not been granted government approval. We are making a case to get that approval granted and would like your assistance.

"I've asked Tony Baxter, who's the lead on this case, to join us to bring you up to speed. Now, I must warn you, Tony is a hothead, but he's top-notch and I think you will like him." He looked down at his phone as he finished off texting Tony and as Betty appeared with Sam's tea.

"That's great, I'm happy to assist. I'm looking forward to

putting my teaching into practice," Sam said.

They heard a knock but before Barry could respond, the door opened, and a head of curly black hair appeared around the door. "I thought I'd let myself in."

"Good, you're here. Come in. Tony, I would like to introduce you to Dr Samantha Page. I have told her you are lead on the McDonnell and Savanna case and I asked you here to fill in Samantha on your approach."

"Pleased to meet you, Samantha. Barry has told me so much about you. Welcome onboard, Professor!" Tony said with a shrewd grin as he shook her hand. His grip was firm and his eyes daring.

"Thank you, Tony. Before you give me a run-down and we talk about strategy, I would first like to ask you some questions about why they didn't get government approval at the hearing. I hope you don't mind?" Sam took a sip of hot lemon tea.

"Nothing really to discuss, they just didn't get approval. We need to discuss my strategy and you need to get an understanding of how they do their business before the next and final hearing, or we don't get another chance," Tony replied, refusing Barry's offer of a hot beverage.

"Look, you are the lead. I'm not interested in your strategy or getting an understanding of how they do business. That's your responsibility. I'm here to help you with the merger and, as you said, we only have one more shot at it, so please indulge me and either give me the documents or tell me why they weren't granted approval or I can't help you," Sam said.

He looked from her to Barry, then when the boss nodded his head, he opened the file he had brought with him, selected a document, and started to read, "Section (35), clause b, of the Commonwealth of Australia Merger Act: Failure to prove shareholders of both parties do not have a conflict of interest."

"Is that it?" Sam asked, putting down her tea.

"Yes, that's what it's got here." He handed her his file.

Sam smiled. "Well, gentlemen, it looks like we've got this next hearing in the bag."

"What makes you say that?" Barry said, sitting upright in his chair.

"In all my research into this area, I have never come across any documentation where approval for such a merger is not granted because they did not comply with only one section. Usually, there is a minimum of about two dozen reasons, but I've seen hundreds on many occasions. This next hearing is only a formality. This is all but approved. All you need to do is to comply with the one section and it's done. It's that easy." She returned the file to Tony.

"My understanding is that whether it involves one or one hundred areas of noncompliance the entire hearing starts again," Tony said with false confidence.

"That's what they want you to believe, but that's incorrect. Just comply with this section and it's done. Did you know your clients can ask the government for assistance to help them to comply?" Sam said.

"How?" Barry asked, looking at Tony.

"If the director of either of the two companies involved in the merger puts a request for assistance in writing to the government, they will respond in writing with the best way to get it done. Then, if they still need help, they can arrange for a government official to visit their location and assist them to comply. How about that?" Sam showed them where that was stated in the Australian Competition and Consumer Commission guidelines.

"The ACCC guidelines, absolutely. We are going to get along just fine, Professor." Tony walked over to Sam and shook her hand once again.

"We are off to a great start." Barry looked satisfied.

CELEBRATION DINNER

Walking into her new apartment after picking up some groceries from the local supermarket on her way home, Sam should have been congratulating herself on a successful first day at her new job.

If that was not enough, she had managed to purchase her opulent apartment outright. But she had no time to rest on her laurels; she needed to read the court hearing transcripts for the case her new boss had tasked her with, after telling him it was nothing she couldn't handle.

Sam needed some time to get used to the size and splendour of the place—spacious four-bedroom, two-bathroom apartment with open plan living that she had finally moved into after waiting four weeks for her interior designer to furnish and decorate it.

On her way to her bedroom, she barely noticed the spectacular city views. Positioned on the thirty-fifth level, the view was undoubtedly breathtaking, but she was disappointed that she had been outbid and had missed out on purchasing the penthouse overlooking the Harbour Bridge and Opera House, with its own private glass elevator. Plus, she hated that this apartment was only one level above an entire floor of office spaces.

She had no time to spare if she was going to get changed and meet Billy at their favourite Italian restaurant near his apartment at 7:30 p.m. He'd been trying to arrange a celebration dinner for the last couple of weeks and she owed it to him to be there on time.

She felt more guilty than ever for ignoring him, not only during the last two years due to her university commitments, but over the last few weeks. That was now in the past and at dinner, she planned to tell him that he would be her priority from that night onward.

She was so grateful for his support and patience and for helping her with all the tasks she'd set out for him, from paying bills to retrieving things for her that she'd left in his apartment, sometimes even during his work hours.

This thought horrified her as she was applying her makeup. She quickly washed her face, re-applied it, and raced off to catch the Manly ferry.

——————

"Hi, sweetheart. How was your day?" Billy asked with arms open wide as he sauntered over from the restaurant door.

"I love you, honey." Sam fell into his embrace.

He frowned. "Hey, what's going on. What happened?"

"Nothing. I'm being silly. I'm just happy to see you."

"Come on, Sam. What's going on? Tell me what's up, please! Did something happen at work?"

"Nothing, honestly. I'm just sorry I haven't been around very much for you and you do so much for me. I don't know how you have put up with my shit over the last couple of years." She fell silently back in his arms.

"Hey, stop that, sweetheart. Don't worry, I haven't done anything I didn't want to do. I'm with you and I do those things for you because I love you." Billy held her tightly. "No more tears now, because tonight we're celebrating."

Once they were seated, Sam slipped off to the bathroom to fix her makeup again while Billy ordered their drinks. The restaurant was busy for a Monday night, but it was summer and the start of the school holidays, so Sam suspected they were lucky to get a table without a booking.

"I've ordered the wine. Are you alright, sweetheart?" he asked.

"Sorry about that, honey. I'm so sorry for everything over the last few years. It's just hit me, and I don't know how you put up with it all this time!" She couldn't start crying again. There were only so many times in one day she could fix her makeup.

The waiter arrived with their bottle of wine and poured them both a full glass and promised to come back shortly and take their meal orders.

"Enough of that, tonight is all about you, Sam—a celebration of an incredible accomplishment. Did you know that you started uni in early 2014, completed your bachelor's degree twelve months later, and immediately commenced a PhD? If that wasn't enough, you became a university lecturer and bloody completed your PhD eighteen months later. Who does that? Dr Samantha Page, I may not be a scholar, but I know this is unheard of.

"Then you got a six-month full-time teaching spot at the same uni. And now you've started a fancy new job and moved into your new apartment. That's sensational, Sam! Yes, 2017 has been a huge year for you. A toast to Dr Samantha Page, the woman who can do anything!"

"How did you remember all that?" Sam blushed and laughed.

"It was easy because I'm so proud of you. But now I'm starving so let's get something to eat." His stomach rumbled.

They both laughed and opened their menus and, when their waiter returned, placed their orders. As they enjoyed their wine and just spending time together, Sam made a promise that she would have every weekend dedicated to him without fail.

As they walked hand-in-hand out of the restaurant, Billy said, "Let's take a walk along the beach, sweetheart."

"It's Monday. I need to get back home for an early start tomorrow," she said regretfully, placing her hand on the side of his face.

"I understand; it's a new job. I'm sorry for arranging this on a Monday night." He kissed her palm.

"Why are you apologising? I should be apologising! Remember, starting this weekend, I'm going to spoil you. Just you wait and see. Walk me to the ferry and I'll tell you what I'm going to do to you." She pulled him towards the wharf.

As they walked to the ferry, they discussed how they would pleasure each other in her new apartment on the weekend. He seemed surprised by her renewed focus on him but pleased.

On her return to her apartment, Sam got straight into her reading and didn't stop for three hours. It was almost midnight when she put the book glasses away and got ready for bed, after setting an alarm on her phone for 6:30 a.m.

The next morning, she was impressed with herself for making it in to work in forty minutes. Ten faster than the previous day.

"Good morning, Dr Page. Sorry to disturb you but I came in early to meet you. Hi, I'm your personal legal secretary, Joanne Lewis," a young woman announced cheerfully. She was petite with soft brown eyes and an open face.

"Hi, Joanne. Please call me Sam. Come in. How are you?" She got up from behind her desk and walked over to her.

"Good, thanks. Welcome onboard. I've heard so much about you and I'm looking forward to working for you."

"Thank you. Have you been working here long?" Sam asked, looking her up and down.

"Yes, nearly ten years now. I'm up from conveyancing. I hope you don't mind, but I must ask you, I need this Friday off, please. I'm picking up my parents from the airport. They are flying in from Brisbane and staying over for the weekend."

"Yes, of course, Joanne., Anything else I can help you with, please let me know."

"You are too kind, Sam. Thank you. I'll be in the front office if you need me and I'll also be handling all your incoming calls. Can I get you a tea or coffee?"

"I can get my own tea and coffee, Joanne. Thank you anyway."

"I don't mind. Are you sure?"

"I'm sure. I have a huge pile of documents I need you to file away for me please, so you can start on those. And, Joanne, I'm really looking forward to working with you," Sam said while walking her out the door.

———

Around morning teatime, Sam was in the boardroom in a senior staff meeting when Joanne walked in and whispered in her ear, "There are two police officers in your office."

Sam immediately stood up, excused herself and followed her back to her office. "Do you know why they're here?"

"No, they just asked for you."

"Hello, I'm Samantha Page. How can I help you?" Sam said as she walked into her office.

"Hello, Dr Page, I'm Senior Constable Larry Bennett and this is Constable Martha Brently. We are from Manly Police

Station. Sorry to interrupt your work, ma'am. It took us a while to track you down."

She looked them up and down. The two constables were as well-built and bulky as she would have expected, but it was the look on their faces that brought about the whisper of nerves. It was a while since Sam had felt that way. "Yes, this is only my second day working here," she said, trying to smile.

"Yes, Professor Grasim from Sydney University told us we could find you here. Ma'am, we regret to inform you that William Ashley was attacked last night while walking home. An ambulance was called but, I'm sorry, he was pronounced dead on arrival at the Manly Hospital."

As Sam buckled and dropped to the floor, he said, "Martha, quick, call an ambulance. She's fainted."

NOT BILLY!

"Dr Page, it's okay, you've just fainted. You're in your office and we would like to take you to St Vincent's Hospital for a check-up as a precaution," the paramedic said as he took her vital signs.

"What happened?" Sam asked, still hazy. It all came back to her when she sat up and saw the police officers. "Not Billy. No, not *Billy!*" Sam sobbed, her heart breaking into pieces.

"Do we have your permission to take you to the hospital for a check-up, Dr Page?" the paramedic asked.

"No, I'm okay. I just need to sit down for a while," she said between sobs as tears streamed down her face. The paramedic helped her up off the floor and walked her over to her chair behind her desk. "Can you tell me where Billy is, please?"

"The police officers are still here. I'll go get them for you."

"Ma'am, we can take you to identify the body," Senior Constable Bennett said when he came back into her office.

"How do you know it's my Billy?"

"His driver's licence was in his wallet as was your picture."

Sam looked at Barry, who was standing just inside her

office looking concerned but helpless. He caught her eye. "Go and do what you need to do. Take whatever time you need."

Distraught and heartbroken, she turned to the police officer. "Okay, thank you."

"Certainly, ma'am," he replied respectfully.

"Have his parents been notified?" Sam asked after gathering herself and looking around frantically for her glasses.

"I can find out for you." He asked his partner to call in to let Manly Hospital know they were on their way with Dr Page.

"My glasses, I can't find my glasses!" said Sam.

"I've got them, Dr Page, here you go." The paramedic handed them to her. "I took them off while I was conducting my examination. They're very fancy."

"Thank you. They're a family heirloom," she explained with a sick feeling in her stomach.

The two officers escorted her out of her office into a full room of silent, staring staff, but she barely noticed any of them.

She found herself in the back of a police car on the way to do the unimaginable. She struggled to contain herself and, when it was confirmed that Billy's parents had not yet been contacted, she broke down again and sobbed.

When they arrived at Many Hospital, Sam was barely holding herself together and the shock of seeing Billy's lifeless body was so overwhelming that the hospital duty doctor administered a mild sedative.

By the time the police officers got her back to her apartment and settled her on the lounge, she had come out of her numb state and thanked them for driving her home. When she closed the door on them, she burst into tears and sobbed until her tears ran out.

***

It was a few days later, after ignoring many knocks on the door, phone calls and text messages, she decided to answer a knock that was a little more aggressive and persistent than the others. Still in her nightwear and looking like a zombie, she opened the door.

"Sam, you okay, darling?" Sister Sue said, bursting into tears.

"Oh, Sister Sue, Billy is gone. He's dead!" Sam cried.

"I know, darling, I know. I just found out and I'm sorry for taking so long to get here to see you, but you are a hard person to find, my darling." Still in the doorway, Sister Sue embraced Sam with tears streaming down her face.

"How did you find me?"

"Professor Grasim told me where to find you."

"Please come in!" Sam almost dragged her inside and closed the door.

"Oh, my goodness, Sam." Sue gaped at the opulence of her new apartment.

"Yes, I know. It's a little over the top, isn't it?"

"A little over the top is an understatement. It's the lifestyle of the rich and famous."

"Thank you for coming, Sue. I really need to talk to you."

"What happened to Billy? I was watching the news and they showed his photo and said he was attacked by three men on his way home to his apartment. I was shocked when they said they'd killed him. Why would anyone kill such a good boy?"

Sam froze. "Did you say three men?"

"That's what they said on the news."

Her mind raced. Three men... "All I know from the police is that he was attacked near his apartment, that's it. What else did they say on the news?"

"Witnesses spotted three men dragging Billy into a street

near his apartment and he was later found by a shopkeeper. Oh, Sam, I'm so sorry."

"I don't know what I'm going to do without him, Sue. That kind of love only ever comes once in a lifetime." Sam fell into her arms.

After holding her for a few minutes, Sister Sue pulled away. Sam was surprised by the resolute look on her face. "Sam, look at me, my darl—" She stopped short when the doorbell began to ring nonstop.

Startled, they went to the door and opened it.

The two police officers who had notified her about Billy were standing outside. "Sorry to trouble you again, Dr Page. Can we come in, please?" asked the senior officer.

"Yes, come in. This is Sister Sue," Sam said.

"Hello, Sister. I'm Senior Constable Larry Bennett and this is Constable Martha Brently from Manly Police Station," he said as they walked in.

"You have a beautiful home, ma'am," Officer Brently said while placing her folder on the coffee table.

"Why didn't you tell me three men killed him? It's all over the TV," Sam asked.

He frowned. "It was early in the investigations and we didn't want to tell you until we had the facts and yes, you are right, three men have been identified by witnesses and we have confirmed that with CCTV," he said.

"And what have you done about it?" Sam asked.

Senior Constable Bennett stood up. "That's why we are here, to tell you that the three suspects have been arrested. We will be charging them later today with the murder of William Ashley."

Sam choked back tears. "Thank you, thank you so much."

The following few weeks were a blur for Sam. Being without Billy sent her to that dark place that was all too familiar from her childhood. It was as if his killers had taken her life as well as his. She felt broken beyond repair. The road she had travelled had changed her in a way she wasn't sure she fully understood.

But she knew one thing—Billy's killers wouldn't get away with it.

That meant she had to snap out of it. She needed to make sure they paid for his death and she would make sure it hurt.

IT'S MY BUSINESS

Late one afternoon, Sam received a text from Barry Stanley requesting she call him urgently.

After some small talk, Barry got to the point of his call. "I have a friend, a well-known businessman, who's fallen on hard times after his marriage failed and his health took a bad turn. He is looking for a business partner who is trustworthy, honest and smart, and you were the first person I thought of."

Despite the dead feeling that was constant since Billy had died, Sam couldn't deny she was flattered. "I'll have to think about it."

"Will you at least meet with him? He's happy to come to your apartment if it's easier for you. I can bring him over."

Sam barely thought about the meeting until 9 a.m. approached and she went to welcome her guests into her home.

"Good morning, Samantha. Oh sorry, Dr Page. I'd like to introduce you to Malcolm Sutton," Barry said as they stepped into her apartment.

Standing over six-foot-tall with intelligent hazel eyes and short jet-black hair that must have been dyed, Malcolm Sutton was a man she felt strangely comfortable with, despite having just met him. "Hello, gentlemen. Welcome," Sam said politely.

"Pleased to meet you, Dr Page," Sutton said, looking at her up and down. He seemed surprised at how young she was; a reaction that she saw all too often.

"Please call me Sam. Come into the boardroom where I have arranged to have morning tea. Would you like tea or coffee?" She walked them inside.

"Sam, what a beautiful home you have. I'll have coffee, please. Two sugars and milk, thanks," Sutton replied as he looked around.

They all took a seat, then, prompted by Barry, she gave the men a swift rundown on how she had got to be where she was without giving away too much detail. It was enough to make Sutton talk, and, after almost two hours of a comprehensive breakdown of his business, Sam was impressed by the genuine quality of the man. He reminded her of how she'd always imagined her real father.

"Mr Sutton, I have no experience whatsoever in the mining industry, so I don't think I would be of any help to you. In fact, given my lack of knowledge of the industry, I could even end up doing you further harm," she said.

"Are you familiar with Australian business law?" asked Sutton.

"Yes, sir."

"Do you have access to and are you prepared to invest five million dollars for a fifty percent share of Sutton Global?" he asked, his gaze direct.

"Possibly."

"Okay, then ask yourself, would you be able to work with me?"

She smiled. "I don't know you."

"Well, that makes two of us. Come on board and let's get to

know each other and help me grow the business. Times have changed and I need someone with young, fresh eyes. I believe your business law knowledge will give us an edge that we very much need. I don't have children and would love to have someone to whom I could pass on all my knowledge and experience. What do you say?"

Barry may have looked shocked, but Sam controlled her expression. "I'm sorry, Mr Sutton, I can't give you an answer right now. I'll need time to think about it."

"You know, Sam, for someone so young, you are very wise. It has been a pleasure meeting you. Before you make up your mind, I would like you to come and visit my coal mine in Western Australia. Would you at least do that for me?" Sutton asked.

"Sure, when?"

"I'm going back tomorrow morning. Come with me on my private plane and I will fly you straight back to Sydney afterwards and have you home the next day."

"Okay, sure." She shook his hand.

"Malcolm, what do you think about her age now?" Barry asked.

"She may look young, Barry, but she is a wise old soul. I like that. I like that very much indeed!" Sutton replied, looking at Sam.

"I knew you two would get along right from the start," Barry said with a laugh.

"Thanks, Barry," Sam said and shook his hand as well. "This way, gentlemen." She walked them back to the door.

"It's been a pleasure meeting you, Sam, and I will see you tomorrow. I'll have a car pick you up around 8:30 a.m. Our flight is due to leave at 9:30 a.m. with an estimated arrival time in Perth of 12:30 p.m. Don't worry, I'll have you back here before the sun goes down the next day, okay? If you change your mind or any unexpected problem arises, please call me. You have my business card." Sutton's new-found enthusiasm showed with every word.

"No problem. Looking forward to it. Thank you, gentlemen," Sam said as she closed the door.

She was taken by Sutton's invitation to go and see his coal mining operation outside Perth. It had provoked her interest, but what impressed her the most was the man himself.

He was a true gentleman, polite and respectful, and she loved his calmness. His two-piece bespoke black suit and everything about him conveyed wealth without shouting it. He was from old money and had fallen on hard times and his company needed an injection of cash to stay afloat until he could offload his raw material for the best price.

Sam knew that five million dollars was a steal for fifty percent of his business and if she didn't take up the offer, someone else would.

But the meeting, coming so soon after losing Billy, had taken a lot out of her, so she lay down on the couch to rest, hoping to get rid of her headache.

She was surprised when the doorbell buzzed. Her mouth dropped open at the sight of the two people standing in her doorway.

"Hello ma'am, remember us—Detective Terry Roth and Detective Jason Gower?"

"Yes, I do. How did you find me?" Sam replied, remembering them from her time at the museum. They had been looking into Mr Harman's death, the event that had changed the course of her life. She was relieved she had concealed the book glasses.

"Can we come in?" the detective asked politely.

"Yes, of course."

"Wow, look at the view. You certainly have done well for yourself," Detective Roth said, looking around.

"This is amazing; a huge difference from where we first met you!" Detective Gower said.

"Thank you and yes, it is different. I was fortunate to get a position in an investment company soon after I last saw you both and got lucky with the stock market then I took a break from work to do my PhD. Do you like it?" She smiled, hoping to disarm them. If they were here about the glasses... And if they weren't, why had they come?

"You've done well for yourself, Dr Page," Detective Roth said.

"Thank you. Please come and take a seat." She led them to the kitchen table.

"You definitely have more than one chair at your kitchen table, compared to when we last met!" Detective Gower said in astonishment.

"Yes, I do now." Sam laughed to keep calm.

It didn't take long for the detective to get down to business. "Ma'am, we have some developments regarding the Holy Book Glasses, and it was imperative we tell you immediately as we believe your life may be in danger."

"What do you mean?" Sam said as she took a seat next to the detectives.

"Manly Police contacted us after questioning the three men, now on remand, charged with the murder of William 'Billy' Ashley," he continued.

"Our condolences for your loss, ma'am," said Detective Roth.

"Further cross-examinations revealed that Billy wasn't the target, you were. And we believe you still are."

Sam wasn't surprised but put on a convincing display.

"They murdered my Billy because they were after me? It doesn't make sense."

"Ma'am, it is clear to us that they believe you have the Holy Book Glasses and were going to use Billy to lure you in. After reviewing the local street shopfront CCTV footage, we confirmed he was struck down after trying to escape. Ma'am, do you have the Holy Book Glasses?" Detective Gower asked bluntly.

"No, of course not. As I told you before, I don't know anything about them." Sam let the tears come. They needed to believe that her thoughts were only with Billy. Shock and dismay, that's what they had to witness.

"Sorry, ma'am. I needed to ask you," Detective Gower said. The sympathy in his eyes was reassuring.

"I'm sorry, I miss him so much. I don't know how I'm going to live without him!" Sam may have been lying about the book glasses, but her tears for Billy were genuine and heartfelt, so it wasn't that hard to stage a convincing display.

"Ma'am, it is clear from interviews with the men who killed Billy that you have been targeted and whoever hired them is not going to stop pursuing you. We have good reason to believe an organised crime syndicate called Borgata is behind all this. They appear to be heavily invested in retrieving the Holy Book Glasses. The head of the organisation, Antonios Garza, recently arrived in Sydney. I don't understand why they are targeting you, but they will not stop until they get what they are after."

"Why me? I do have reading glass to help with my dyslexia, but why would they think that I have the glasses they're after?" Sam said.

"For whatever reason, ma'am, they will stop at nothing," Detective Roth said. "By the way, can we take a look at your glasses, please, just to rule them out?"

"What glasses?" Sam asked wiping her tears.

"You just told us you have reading glasses to help with your dyslexia," Detective Gower reminded her.

"Oh, yes. I'll go get them." Sam ran to the bedroom and retrieved the spare pair of glasses she'd had made in preparation for this. "Here you go."

"Wow, they are a unique pair, aren't they? I've never seen a metal silver frame like this before. But no, they are not the Holy Book Glasses."

"If the three men are in jail, why do I need to be worried?" Sam asked. She needed as much information as she could get from them.

"A contract was put out on you with instructions to retrieve the Holy Book Glasses. It is only a matter of time before they catch up to you," Gower said as he handed back her spare glasses.

"So, what are the police doing about this?"

"We have people in place and are tracking their every move, but we need your cooperation."

She could see his eyes penetrating her, looking for anything. She tried to appear as pliable as possible. The closer she could get to them, the more she could find out about this syndicate. "Yes, sure. What do you want me to do?"

"If you are contacted by anyone either by phone or in person, you must contact us immediately. Here are our cards again. It's also imperative you keep in contact with us daily, okay? We will do the rest," Gower said.

"Ma'am, if you help us, we can get them and this will be all over, okay?" Roth said.

She smiled. "I can do that."

"We'll see ourselves out, ma'am. If we have anything further, we will be in touch. Again, sorry for your loss," Gower said as they both got up and headed for the door.

Sam locked the door behind them and sat back down with too many questions racing around in her mind. She was aware that they knew a lot more than they were telling her, but she didn't dwell on the missed opportunity. Instead, she focused her energy on finding out more about Borgata and Antonios Garza.

She changed into something more casual and headed to the university library to find out more about the bent and twisted individual who had ordered the retrieval of the glasses and the contract on her that had led to Billy's death.

Methodically and calmly, Sam spent hours researching with zero results. Frustrated, she selected the latest military tactics and combat training, martial arts, and tactical espionage training methodology research papers to bring herself up to date with what she would need when this monster finally caught up with her.

But she was determined to control even the time and location by allowing him to find her when she was ready. Garza and his cronies would be in for a nasty surprise when they tried to come after her.

———

As soon as Sam returned to Sydney the next day, she discussed Sutton's offer with Barry. Having received endorsements regarding her decision, she phoned Sutton late Wednesday afternoon and verbally sealed the deal.

On her return from Western Australia, she had verified the numbers supplied by Sutton and reviewed his background and business dealings. She was surprised to find no liability or bad credit. He obviously knew how to conduct business. How then, had his company come to such a low?

She recalled that, a few years before, she had been struggling to survive and unable to prepare for a job interview and now she was living in a luxury penthouse and preparing for a multimillion-dollar business deal. She was in awe of the heights, both metaphorically and physically, to which she had risen in such a short period, but clearly, even the brightest of people could descend in some cases. She would do her best to ensure it didn't happen to her.

Joy turned to despair that she couldn't share this with Billy.

Not wanting to wallow in the past, she snapped out of her reverie and continued to prepare her business documents. She didn't need a lawyer; she used to teach this to lawyers, and she prepared a document that was rock solid in every way. Sutton, on the other hand, had a team of lawyers, which mean that it took him a week to sign it.

Once the contract was signed, Sam wasted no time in transferring the money. With cashflow re-established for the payroll, productivity instantly increased, along with yield of the material. Sutton & Page Global was on its way. She leased the floor below her apartment as office space and began to work on the business in earnest.

WHO'S THE BITCH NOW?

Within a few weeks the coal mine had picked up and trade was lucrative. Sam didn't hesitate to take advantage of the stock market and soon share prices began to soar as investors recognised Sutton & Page Global as a new force in the industry.

She was now proficient at self-defence and decided to set up a training room next to her office on the floor below so that her instructor could come around more regularly. There was always more to be learned.

She also joined a gun club and started target practise. Australian firearms laws had made joining the club a necessity as that was a valid reason to own a firearm. Protecting yourself was not, and revenge was way off the cards. So, she had happily accepted her provisional 12-month pistol license citing her new-found enthusiasm for target shooting. She had worried that they might ask too many questions or look into her records and refuse her because of Billy's death, but that hadn't happened, fortunately.

She was determined to set her plans for retribution in motion. While Sutton & Page Global continued to grow, Sam directed the book glasses to focus on the task to identify, locate and destroy not only the lower-level Borgata thugs, but their boss, the man behind Billy's death, Antonios Garza.

After a good night's sleep, she spent the next day reading, ensuring she took regular breaks. The following day, after breakfast and a shower, she dressed in her gym gear that included a waist pack in which she placed the book glasses, the spare glasses, her keys, and a credit card. She strapped her mobile phone to one arm, then attached cordless earphones and put on a running cap and sunglasses before setting off for the crime scene.

Sam set a quick pace as she ran through the city crowd to the Quay. She'd taken up running even before Billy had died as it helped to manage the side effects from the glasses. She had come to realise that she felt better for it and slept better. Before she'd started running and working out at the gym, lack of sleep had been her biggest downfall and, without sleep, she lacked the concentration to glean the full benefits of the book glasses.

As she approached the Quay, she slowed her pace and came to a stop at the ticketing booth on the wharf, where she purchased her ticket using her credit card.

There was no time for sightseeing on the ferry trip over to Manly; her focus was set on the task ahead, going over various attack and exit strategies.

After disembarking at Manly Wharf, Sam ran directly to Billy's apartment, hoping to be spotted by replacement Borgata thugs or perhaps even the big boss himself. As she unlocked the door, out of the corner of her eye she saw a man approach her and felt something like a knife being pressed into her back.

A man in a black ski mask stood there holding a knife with a long blade. "Where are the fucking glasses, bitch?" he asked in a sophisticated English accent.

She kept her hands up as she turned to face him. As he

stepped closer to her, she took the knife out of his hands with a twist, turn and a flick of force he wasn't expecting. Once he was off-balance, she jumped on his back and smashed his face into the floor, hard.

While he was dazed, Sam punched holes with the knife into both shoulder blades before stabbing the back of both of his legs. "Who's the bitch now?" Sam said, with the knife pressed to his neck. "I'm only going to ask you once—tell me about Borgata!"

"Borgata is a business run by a powerful man," he said, groaning.

"This powerful man's name is Antonios Garza, is that correct?"

"Yes!"

"Where can I find him?" She pressed the knife even harder into his neck when the man hesitated.

"He's here in Sydney." The masked man was weakening.

"Where in Sydney?" Sam knew she was running out of time.

"The eightieth floor of the Four Seasons Hotel," he said, breathing heavily.

Before she had a chance to respond she heard someone approach but didn't move off the back of the masked man and kept the knife pressed to his neck.

"Police—drop the knife and put your hands up!"

She looked up to see the two plainclothes detectives approaching, so she dropped the knife and raised her hands. One of them kicked the knife away and grabbed her while the other surveyed the masked man's wounds.

Then they turned their attention to Sam and immediately recognised her.

"Samantha Page? Did you do this?" Detective Roth yelled. "What the hell?"

While Detective Gower called it in, Detective Roth took Sam into the kitchen, handcuffed her, and sat her down. It wasn't until the ambulance had taken the masked man away that the two detectives turned to her.

"What happened? What are you doing here?" Detective Roth asked.

Tears were again her friends. "What do you mean, what am I doing here? This is my apartment! I half-owned it with Billy. It's been hard for me to come back here since his murder and today I finally built up enough courage to come back. Just after I unlocked the door someone held a knife to my back. I turned around and that's when I saw the masked man. I started to walk backwards, and he came after me, but the idiot tripped and fell flat on his face and dropped the knife. So, I grabbed it and jumped on his back and that's when you both arrived and found me."

"How did he get the knife wounds on both his legs and shoulders?" Detective Roth asked.

"Well, he's a big boy, I needed to keep him down. If you don't believe me, just ask him."

"Take the cuffs off," Gower said, and Roth immediately complied.

"You were very lucky, Dr Page," said Gower. "What were you thinking, taking on someone like that?"

"I was so mad when I saw him. I thought he might have been one of the men who killed Billy, so when he fell, I took my chances. I wasn't thinking," Sam said. "I thought he was going to kill me next."

"I suggest you don't react in the same way next time something like this happens. It's best you run and not confront these sorts of people. Leave it to the police." Gower looked disturbed. "We'll need to take a statement, but after that, you'll be able to go. Are you okay to get home by yourself, ma'am?"

"Yes, I'll be fine. I need to run all this adrenaline off anyway. But I'm going to stay and clean up here first, so please don't wait for me." Sam kept on with the charade.

"You'll have to wait until we have a statement for you to check," Gower said.

"Of course."

It was hours before they all left, having taken their statement and photos of the blood splatters on her clothes and skin.

After they had gone, it was getting dark and too late to go running on her own, so she decided to stay there for the night. After ordering dinner, she scrubbed the remaining blood from her hands and arms as she planned out a visit to the Four Seasons Hotel on her way home the following day.

Sam hardly touched her dinner. It was Billy's favourite, and she had ordered for two out of habit. After eating only a few spoonfuls, she wrapped it back up and placed it in the fridge. She hid the book glasses in her old hiding spot in Billy's apartment. She would make sure she took them with her before she left.

Overcome with weariness, she dragged herself into the bedroom and slid in-between the cool sheets. She inhaled deeply and quickly drifted off, dreaming of how Billy would call her sweetheart.

FOUR SEASONS HOTEL

Waking up in the middle of the night, Sam looked over and noticed on the clock on the bedside table displayed 3:14 a.m. Noticing she was still fully dressed and even wearing her runners, she got up to get a drink of water.

Before she reached the bedroom door, she was grabbed from behind and pulled off balance into a solid muscular torso. The last thing she noticed was a wet cloth placed over her mouth and a chemical smell before she blacked out.

———

"Wake up, wake up, sleeping beauty. Dr Page, I'm glad to finally meet you. I have had such a terrible time finding you, but all is forgiven now that you're here."

A well-dressed man in an immaculate three-piece blue pinstripe suit stood over her in the middle of a room elegantly decorated with mahogany wood detail and rich silks.

"Where am I and who are you?" Sam asked, still feeling groggy. She wondered what they'd used on her.

"You are in my suite at the Four Seasons, my dear. Let me introduce myself. My name is Antonios Garza. I'm the director of Borgata. you may call me Director."

At first, Sam thought he spoke with an English accent but after hearing it for the second time, it was clear to her that it was a mixture of English and Italian. It created a distinct sound with his unusual low tone.

Pain in her wrists drew her attention to the fact the ties binding her hands were digging into them. She was tied to a chair in the middle of the room. When she tried to move her feet, she realised her ankles were also secured to the chair legs. Whoever had tied her up had done a good job of immobilising her—too good a job.

Initially, she'd thought she was alone with Garza, but when she swivelled her head around to scan the room, she discovered two of his stony-faced thugs, one behind her left shoulder and another behind her right.

Sam's thinking became clearer by the minute as the fog in her brain dissipated. But she needed to buy more time to more fully recover from the drug's effects if she were to have any chance of escape. "How did you get me up here?"

"I have a private elevator that leads from my suite directly to my vehicle in the basement car park. I'm afraid no one saw you arrive, and no one will see you leave.

"Enough of your questions; I don't play games. You will not find me toying with you, Page. This is not anything like what you young people see in the movies. This is real life, and in real life, people die, just like Billy.

"I killed him and I'm going to kill you, now tell me where the glasses are." He turned his back on her and walked over to the huge window to look out over a magnificent view of Sydney Harbour.

"You murdered my Billy. For that, I will kill you!" Sam screamed, her fury rising in response to his casual confession.

"You amuse me. I see your pain; it is clear to me. And I will end your suffering; it will not be long. Just give me the glasses and I will end your suffering now." He voice was strangely inviting and almost calming.

"Not if I end you first!"

The door to the suite crashed open and in rushed six fully masked police officers dressed in black with their weapons aimed directly at the two thugs flanking Sam, who were both holding long jagged hunting knives.

No sooner did Sam notice three red dots on each of the thugs' chests, she heard many gunshots almost deafening her. She closed her eyes as if that would magically protect her from the bullets flying around the room.

When she opened them again, the two thugs were slumped on the floor, unmoving.

"Dr Page, are you all right?" Detective Gower asked while untying her from the chair. "Where's Garza?"

"Over there, in front of the window!"

"Where?" Roth asked.

"Shit, he used the elevator. Quick, his private elevator will take him directly to the basement car park. He'll get away!" Sam called out again in terror.

The officers ran out the door in pursuit of Garza, leaving Sam with the two detectives.

"Sorry we took so long to get here, but they got to our team and by the time we arrived at the apartment, you were gone. Our best guess was to come here and luckily, we did," Gower explained, freeing her from the chair.

"Why didn't you tell us you were staying at the Manly apartment?" Roth asked.

"Well, I didn't intend to stay but it was nearly dark by the time I finished cleaning up. So, I ordered in some dinner and then crashed."

"How did Garza get to you?" Gower asked.

Sam explained the little she remembered after getting out of bed in the middle of the night and then waking up in Garza's hotel suite.

"What did he say to you?" Gower asked, after getting her a glass of water from the kitchen.

"Did he mention the Holy Book Glasses?" Roth asked.

"Yes, and he thinks I have them. Just because I worked at the museum it doesn't mean I have them!" Sam continued to play her role. "And Garza admitted to having Billy killed."

"Can you see what we are talking about now? Garza is convinced you have the Holy Book Glasses, and he is going to continue to kill until he gets them," Roth said.

"I don't have them. How many times must I tell you!" Sam was faultless in her consistent denial.

"Okay, okay, but look at what lengths they are going to get to you. Whether you have them or not, they will not stop until you are dead. I suggest you don't leave your apartment unaccompanied. I will have a uniformed police officer stationed outside your door twenty-four-seven," Gower said.

"Come on, we need to take you to the hospital to have you checked over." Roth helped her up from the chair and to the front door.

She submitted to the hospital visit at St Vincent's Hospital, detectives beside her, and let them check her out.

Finally, the doctor smiled as she noted Sam's pulse on her chart. "I'm happy to inform you that apart from the bump on your head and a few bruises and grazes, you and your baby are perfectively fine. Nothing to worry about."

THE PENTHOUSE SUITE

Sam reached out and grabbed hold of the doctor's arm. "Baby? What baby? I'm not pregnant, I can't be. I have no symptoms."

"You are most definitely pregnant. I'm guessing you are about nine or ten weeks? Some mothers don't have any obvious signs early in their pregnancy. If you haven't yet, don't worry, that will come sooner or later. Just speak to your doctor about it, okay? You are fine to leave at any time you feel ready, take care," the doctor said before exiting the cubicle.

Speechless, Sam sat up on the edge of the bed with her legs dangling over the side.

"Congratulations, Dr Page. Let's see, we're now in October, so that makes it a May baby," Gower said as he walked up to her and stood directly in front of her.

She shed some tears and abruptly slumped onto the detective, shocked that she couldn't control her emotions and missing Billy more than ever.

Gower put his arms around her. "What a wonderful surprise. Take this gift and don't look back."

Without a word, Roth took a seat next to the bed and

waited patiently for her to recover from her surprise so they could take her home again.

"Sorry about that. I'm fine now." She wiped away her tears.

Gower handed her the tissue box sitting next to the bed. "When you are ready, we would like to take you home."

"Sure, thanks. But can we go back to Billy's apartment first? I left some personal items and I need to get them," Sam said casually to avoid raising suspicion.

Roth shot up from his seat. "I don't think it's a good idea."

She hopped off the bed. "Look, I need to go back sometime soon and get my things and I would feel so much safer going back with you. Please? I won't take long."

Reluctantly, the two detectives escorted her over to the Manly apartment and they were all in and out in less than two minutes. As they got back into the detectives' vehicle, Roth reached over and took the backpack in which Sam had packed the few things she had gathered from the apartment and searched it for the Holy Book Glasses.

Sam didn't object to his search as she had hidden the glasses in her bra before exiting the bedroom.

The detectives remained silent all the way back to her apartment. Once there, they introduced her to their colleague, Detective Taylor, and explained that each new detective assigned to protective duty would always start a conversation with a password. That way she could identify any detective as someone legitimately assigned to protect her.

"What's the password?" Sam asked.

"Come inside the apartment and I'll tell you," Gower said. They all walked into her apartment and he locked the door behind them. "The password is 'caution'."

"Okay, fine," Sam replied and excused herself to go to the bathroom.

Gower, Roth, and Taylor then walked back outside, making

sure to lock the door and, after a short conversation, Gower and Roth left Taylor to stand guard.

———

The next morning, Sam's head was still tender and, although the swelling had gone down, she could still feel a lump. Unusually, she didn't feel like any breakfast and got out the book glasses to read her emails on her laptop.

After grasping the fact that she'd finally got the book glasses back, she stopped and stared at them for a while. Then she wiped her anguished tears from her eyes and proceeded to check her emails.

She didn't know if it was the tears or if the glasses were playing with her mind when she read that the penthouse apartment that she had so desperately wanted but failed to win at auction was now being offered to her and she had ten days to respond if she still wanted it.

After frantically looking at the calendar, she realised that the following day would be the tenth and final day. She excitedly called the real estate agency to confirm she wanted to purchase the penthouse apartment.

After ending the phone call, she transferred the deposit and forwarded an email to the agent, giving her permission to put her current apartment back on the market.

This good news was what she needed to put her in the right frame of mind. But then, without warning, her stomach heaved, and she raced off to the toilet to initiate a morning ritual that would become commonplace over the next few weeks.

———

The following week, Sam visited her GP, who referred her to an obstetrician. Her subsequent move into the penthouse went seamlessly and, with detectives watching over her twenty-four-seven, she had no dramas with Garza.

She wasn't yet showing any sign of a baby bump and continued her exercise routine of self-defence (with certain moves ruled out because of the baby) and regular runs but restricted her gym workouts to treadmills only.

She also went back to work and her private elevator, in addition to stopping at ground and basement car park levels, was configured to stop on the thirty-fourth floor. This meant the added security and convenience of not changing elevators to reach her office, thus avoiding interactions with strangers and unnecessary conversations. This fringe benefit was p7riceless to her and made her love her new penthouse apartment even more.

With a sensational rooftop level in addition to a luxurious two-floor apartment, Sam's penthouse was three levels of sheer opulence that far surpassed her expectations. The transparent glass elevator opened its doors into an awe-inspiring foyer with an unforgettable view. Off the foyer was a boardroom with one wall made of full-length glass windows providing an unob-structed panorama of Sydney Harbour. In the middle of the room sat a magnificent solid oak boardroom table which she simply adored.

After a brief trip to Perth to deal with business with Malcolm, she answered her mobile after noticing Detective Gower was calling. "Hello, Detective."

"Hello, Sam. Just touching base to see how things are going. Are you well?"

"All good, and thanks for understanding regarding my Perth trip."

"Detective Roth told me you are working on a new business venture. I take it the Perth trip was fruitful for you?"

"Yes, it's my business. Well, half of it is. I have a fifty percent partnership and I'm really enjoying it."

"Yeah, the bloody rich get richer, I think," Gower said with a touch of bitterness.

"Now, now, Detective, your claws are showing," Sam said with a laugh.

"On a more serious matter, please keep alert. We have heard through our sources that Garza is renewing his efforts to get at you. So please listen to the detectives and you will be safe. We planned for this and you keeping within your apartment as much as possible helps us manage the situation."

"Will do. I will let you know if I need to leave my apartment, don't worry." Sam replied, not happy at all.

PASSING OF A GREAT MAN

Sam spent the entire weekend with Sister Sue at her apartment. Sue had been shocked, saddened and thrilled at the news of her pregnancy and had assured Sam that she would be there for her through both the highs and lows.

Monday morning started no different from any other but, just after 9 a.m., Sam received a phone call from Malcolm's assistant, Betty Tamis, to inform her that Malcolm Sutton had passed away during the night from a massive heart attack. It was 6 a.m. in Perth and Betty told her she was needed there later that day to sit in on a crucial meeting on his behalf.

Sam was shocked to discover that Malcolm had been in the midst of discussions regarding a takeover bid for Swan Coal Energy, and had a meeting scheduled with their top executives at 1 p.m.

"He was working on this deal before you came on board," Betty explained. "You were the clincher to finally securing the deal. News of the business's turnaround has spread throughout the industry and Swan Coal Energy wanted in on the action."

From what Sam had seen of Swan Coal Energy, if the

merger happened, they would end up a giant within the industry and would earn billions from securing a thirty-year contract to sell coal to China. "Okay, it sounds like a good deal."

"It is," Betty said, her voice turning soft. "Poor Malcolm. He said that this wouldn't have happened without you coming on board. You should have seen his face the day he told me about this deal. It was the happiest I'd seen him for decades."

Sam took a few minutes after the phone call to compose herself before she called Barry to inform him of the passing of his friend. Finally, she updated Gower and promised to continue to phone him daily.

Sam had less than an hour to get to the airport where Malcolm's private jet was standing by to take her to Perth. Betty had thought of everything and had organised the jet hours before talking to her. His assistant was a true gem and Sam knew from the moment they'd met that they would work well together.

Due to Betty's efforts, Sam arrived at the 1 p.m. meeting on time with all the necessary information, which Betty had emailed to her while she was in flight.

Walking into the boardroom at the head office of Sutton & Page Global with less than a minute to spare, she was astonished to note that Swan Coal Energy CEO, Alex Foley, had four lawyers, his PA and two senior company directors with him.

Thanks to Betty, Sam recognised Alex Foley instantly and, after accepting all their condolences, asked to see him privately outside.

"Thank you, Mr Foley, for obliging me. I don't want to embarrass you, sir, but this meeting will only commence if it is in private between the two of us," Sam said.

"I always have my meetings with Malcolm this way!" Foley

said, looking furious.

"I'm not Mr Sutton, sir. And it's up to you. If you refuse to meet in private, then you leave me with no choice but to cancel the meeting indefinitely," Sam said, standing her ground.

He scowled. "I don't like this, missy!"

She didn't break eye contact. "What don't you like, sir? I will not have anyone with me in the meeting either. It will be just the two of us. And, by the way, it's Dr Page, thank you!"

But he wasn't backing down either. "Malcolm told me he hadn't yet read you in on this deal, so I wonder if I'm wasting my time talking to you at all."

"Do you want to hear our offer or not? It's up to you."

"Yeah, okay. But I don't like it. I'm here anyway, so let's hear the offer. Okay, okay, I will get them all to wait in the foyer," he reluctantly conceded.

"Thank you," said Sam before walking back into the boardroom.

Foley asked his entourage to leave the boardroom and he and Sam took a seat opposite each other. Betty walked in with afternoon tea for all the meeting attendees and Sam could barely conceal her amusement when she rolled her eyes in shock upon seeing all of Foley's advisors filing out the door.

"Help yourself, please. Tea or coffee?" Sam politely offered.

"Don't mind if I do." Foley made himself a coffee and sat back with attitude, waiting for her.

Almost ninety minutes later, they emerged from the board-room to find his displeased and impatient entourage still waiting for him in the foyer.

"Thank you, Dr Page. I will get my lawyers to email you everything over," Foley said as he stepped into the foyer. "Come on, team. We need to get back and get ready for this merger. We have a deal!"

"Betty, may I see you in here, please?" Sam called as the office staff stared in silence.

Betty approached Sam, running her hand nervously over her short curly hair. Sam could see her lined hands shaking. "Yes, ma'am. How can I help you?"

"Take a seat next to me. Can you please call me Sam? Would you do that for me?"

"Yes, of course, ma'am, I mean Sam," Betty answered.

"Thank you. I'm happy to inform you that we do have a deal with Mr Foley. Now it's just a matter of getting government approval for the merger to proceed."

"Sam, I love your glasses. They look old and precious." Betty's eyes opened wide behind her glasses as she stared at them.

"Oh yes, they are a family hand-me-down. I have only changed the lenses," Sam said, giving her standard response.

"They certainly are beautiful."

"Thanks, are you curious about the deal?"

"That's not my business," Betty said.

Sam could tell she didn't mean it. "Well, I would like it to be your business. I would like you to be my personal assistant. Malcolm repeatedly told me how lucky he was to have you working with him and I was hoping I could be just as lucky. Would you like to stay on board as my personal assistant?"

Betty burst into tears and Sam gave her a quick hug.

"Tell me about the deal," Betty said, once she had composed herself.

"I got him to agree to all of Malcolm's demands."

"What? Including not staying on as board member?" Betty asked, blinking rapidly.

"That's right, not even as a shareholder."

"Impossible. How?"

"Easy. I told him I had others interested and if he left this meeting, he would not have another chance. He jerked me around with the price, but it's worth it not having him on as a board member or a shareholder, just what Malcolm wanted."

"Malcolm would be proud of you."

"Thank you, Betty, that means a lot to me," Sam said, teary-eyed. "I'm staying until the funeral, so can you please arrange somewhere nearby for me to stay? Also, I will be assisting his estate with all the legal work regarding both Malcolm's business and personal matters. I'm not leaving until I do my best for this great man, but I can't do it without you. Can I rely on you?"

"I'm available for anything!" she replied.

───────

With Malcolm's funeral finally behind her, Sam returned home to Sydney a week later feeling sad, tired, and emotionally drained. The task of assisting with Malcolm's estate had taken its toll, on top of dealing with the details of the merger.

Once back in her apartment, she collapsed on her bed in a heap, desperately seeking out Billy's memory for comfort and as a means of escape. Heartbroken and lonely, she started to feel like the helpless and ignorant loser she had been.

Instantly, she shot up from the bed and put on the book glasses and shook off that frightening thought. She was determined never to return to that dark place where she had been so helpless and lacked any hope for the future.

Recalling her last conversation with the detectives about their department's limited budget for ongoing protection at her apartment, she began an extensive search for a state-of-the-art security firm, the best money could buy, to provide her with round-the-clock protection above and beyond what an average detective could offer.

Sam press send on the email she had written to her new security team to ensure they were keeping their ears to the ground about any further threat from Borgata. Once that was done, she dialled Barry's number.

He answered on the second ring. "To what do I owe this pleasure, Dr Page?"

"Barry, I need you to appoint me a legal team to represent my newly acquired business in a merger. I want four stand-out experts, the best in their fields."

"Page Global, you mean? I've been following what you've had going on. Congratulations."

"Thank you." She tried to remember to smile as she knew it could be heard on the phone. Not that she had to schmooze Barry, and she did like him, but she needed to get the ball rolling on this merger so that there were no delays. If successful, Swan Coal Energy would be incorporated into Page Global, giving Sam the capacity to supply a significant portion of China's coal needs for decades to come and financial domination within the industry. "Can you find me the people I need?"

"Not a problem. I'll put a list together and get it to you in the next few days, okay?"

She swallowed her impatience. "That sounds great."

As she hung up, she reminded herself that getting the best people took time. She knew Barry would give her a decent list, although, even if they were the best, they wouldn't be able to do what she could do.

Never mind. She would keep her hand on things behind the scenes. That should be good enough.

SILVERBACK AND THE TWO THUGS

The glass elevator doors abruptly opened to Sam's apartment and three men in dark suits and a woman in a pin-stripe skirt and a white blouse rushed out.

She saw them through the doorway. "Well, don't just stand there. Come in and take a seat at the conference table."

The four new arrivals quickly took their places and the window shades automatically opened reveal the spectacular city views. Sam viewed them askance from where she sat at the head of the magnificent solid oak timber table, a desk plate of black marble with gold writing in front of her stating: "Dr Samantha Page, CEO—PAGE Global". She hoped they took notice of it.

"Good morning Dr Page," said the group collectively and politely.

"Good morning and thank you for meeting me here today. Look, I'm going to get straight to the point. I want this merger hearing to go smoothly. The acquisition of Western Australia's Swan Coal Energy will give PAGE Global the capacity to supply a significant portion of China's coal needs for decades to come. I have selected each of you based on your outstanding successes. Your firm has assured me of your proven skills in dealing with these types of government hearings.

"As far as I'm concerned, the hearing is only a formality. Let's give them what they want so we can get the green light and move forward as quickly as possible. I will not tolerate anything less than your best. Are we clear?"

"Yes, ma'am!" they replied in unison, each with a self-confident smirk.

"Right. I for one would like to take this opportunity and be the first to wish you a happy birthday, Dr Page," said the man seated the furthest from the head of the table.

She didn't know which one he was. It didn't matter. "Get out, you're fired. Get out now!"

His grin vanished and he made a run for the elevator, in his haste almost knocking over the butler she'd hired to cater for the day as he carried in their drinks.

She leant back, enjoying the fright on the faces of the three who remained. "Look, as you all know I am a lawyer too, and I don't need any of you, but it doesn't look good if I represent my business at this merger review hearing, does it? This is a routine task people, get it done."

"Yes ma'am!" they replied, smirks conspicuously absent.

"If you don't have any questions, you may show yourselves out but leave the briefs on the table." Sam poured herself a lemon tea and waved the butler away.

The remaining three got up, obediently placed their briefs on the table and made their way to the elevator as quietly as possible.

Sam's mobile rang, but she ignored it as she bit into a warm crusty croissant and then sipped on her lemon tea. The phone buzzed and she glanced at the new text message.

Give them back or you too will die, let me in.

Ignoring the message, she flicked the phone to the side of the table and finished her succulent morning tea.

As she put on the book glasses and reached for the brief, the elevator doors opened. She quickly removed the glasses and slipped them into her bra.

"I want the book glasses now, bitch!" yelled a man who resembled a silverback gorilla. He was flanked by two taller thugs with handguns drawn.

"How did you get in?" asked Sam as she walked towards them.

"Give me the fucking book glasses and I will let you live!"

Before he got another word out, Sam kneed him in the groin and thrust her mobile into his larynx, leaving him incapacitated. She pushed him into the two thugs behind him and leapt over them to make her escape via the elevator.

Two terrifyingly loud shots rang out before the elevator door finally closed.

The lift surged downwards to Sam's office on the thirty-fourth floor. The entire floor was secured, so she felt confident she would be safe there.

With the hearing a week away, she was annoyed they had found her, and she feared the worst. She was so close to financial domination and needed just a little more time to see it through.

Silverback and his thugs presented a problem and she certainly didn't need any negative publicity at this crucial point in time. Killing them would be futile as they would only be replaced with who knew what. A deal must be done, she decided, to hold them back until government approval was granted for the merger.

She signed in at the security desk, made her way to her office and hastily locked the door. Then she retrieved the book glasses from inside her bodice and typed a text message:

What assurances do I have?
The reply was almost instantaneous:

Give them back or you will die, let's meet.

OK. *At the museum in one hour.*

OK. *Make sure you bring them.*

She didn't waste any time crossing town to the Australian Museum, leaving her forty minutes to prepare for the negotiation. She hadn't been back there since first starting university. It always evoked fond memories of when she'd first discovered the power of the book glasses.

Despite attempting to suppress her feelings, memories of those days flooded her mind, overwhelming her to the point of feeling slight anxiety about the entire ordeal. It was difficult for her to remember being that frightened and pathetic young woman. It was almost impossible to believe she had ever been that person. She had been presented with a fortuitous and extraordinary opportunity and had grabbed it with both hands and never looked back.

If this were to be the end for her, she was grateful to have experienced the ride of her life over the last five years. Within this short period, she had seen and done things people would not have dreamed of doing in two lifetimes. She had reached great heights, achieved amazing things, and experienced the love her heart had long desired.

And even with her terrible losses, she wasn't ready to give it all up. No, she would work the problem and do whatever she could do to hold them back until the hearing was over. There was no other option while she had the book glasses.

Thursday was a popular day for school tours at the

museum and Sam was able to use the late morning rush to avoid being recognised by any of the museum staff. She made her way to Mr Harman's office and waited for her rendezvous.

As she entered the office, a woman wearing one of the cleaning staff uniforms looked up from where she was polishing the desk.

"Who are you?" Sam asked.

"S-sorry ma'am, M-Mr Robertson is out of the office all day and I t-took the op-opportunity to clean his office, I'm f-finished so I'll g-get out of your way." The woman had a strong Aussie accent.

"Mr Robertson?" asked Sam.

"Yes, M-Mr Robertson, the C-CEO," she said, looking back at Sam oddly.

"Well, Mr Robertson arranged for me to use his office all day, so off you go!" Sam tried to hurry her out.

"Yes ma'am, I-I'll be out of your way as s-soon as I get my cleaning equipment. Have a n-nice day!" She collected her gear and hastily exited the office.

With only minutes to spare, Sam took the fake set of book glasses she'd had made and placed them into the original case and concealed them in the hidden compartment. Then she hid the real set in her bra before taking a seat on the chair behind the CEO's desk.

She heard the step in the corridor outside before she saw the man.

"I see you have returned to the scene of the crime, Page?" It was the man who had confronted her in her apartment—Silverback. He and the two thugs entered the office and closed the door behind them. He took a seat in front of the desk opposite Sam and started to laugh.

"How's the throat? I hope I didn't hurt you too much," Sam said with a grin.

He looked around. "I have fond memories of this office."

"So, you killed Mr Harman here?" Sam said.

He looked satisfied. "Let's not forget about Dr Julie Dunn, shall we? I didn't have the good fortune of getting your boyfriend myself, but you would be happy to know it was my boys who finished him off when he tried to escape. Not fucking smiling now, are you, bitch?"

"When we talked on the phone, you agreed to let me live," Sam said.

"You have them?" he asked, sitting upright, and looking interested.

"No, I don't have them, and I knew you wouldn't believe me, so that's why I wanted to meet you here. The glasses have been in this office all along in a secret compartment. Everyone has searched it, including the police and you as well, and the glasses still haven't been found. I'm the only one who knows where they are. Therefore, if you let me go now, I will text you their precise location after ten minutes."

"And why should I believe a lying bitch like you?"

"Why would I lie? You know where I live!"

He hesitated for a moment and Sam held her breath. "Okay boys, let her out." Then turned to Sam. "You have ten minutes, bitch, and you better not be fucking lying or I'm coming after you."

She took off like the wind and didn't look back. When she arrived at the refuge, she messaged him that the glasses were in the bottom drawer of the office desk, concealed in the false bottom.

The moment the detectives had informed her that Garza had fled back to Italy, she'd put this plan in motion knowing that, by the time the glasses got to Garza and her deceit was revealed, the government hearing regarding approval for the merger would be over. Then she would be free to unleash her fury on Garza and his organisation without fear of being implicated and without endangering the merger.

"Sister Sue, you need to listen to me!" Sam cried as she raced into her office and closed the door behind her.

"Slow down. What's wrong?" Sister Sue asked.

"I need your help. Billy's killers have found me, and I've managed to buy some time but I'm afraid my luck will run out soon!" She took a seat opposite Sue.

"Shush! Lower your voice. We need to go to the police now," Sue said in a loud whisper, and walked around her desk and sat next to Sam.

"I can't go to the police yet."

"Why not?"

"It is complicated. I just need to wait a week before I go to them."

Sue looked confused but she didn't ask awkward questions. "What do you want from me?"

"I need you to wait until I tell you before you call Detective Gower and Detective Roth for me. When the time comes, I will need you to inform them of my location."

"These people killed Billy, my darling. Don't play with fire!" Sue said, her eyes reflecting the fear she felt for Sam.

"I know, but it's complicated. That's why I need your help to get the police involved when the time is right. Can you help me, please?" Sam pleaded.

"I'm not happy with this and I don't know what you are up to, but what is it you want me to do?" Sue replied.

Sam breathed a sigh of relief. "Thank you. Here are the mobile numbers for Detective Gower and Detective Roth. When I message you my location next week, I would like you to call them immediately and tell them that I'm in danger of being killed and need immediate assistance." Sam smiled as she wrote down the numbers for Sue.

"I don't know why you're smiling. The fact you are in so much danger is breaking my heart, my darling. I trust you, but I hope you know what you are doing," Sue said.

"I promise nothing will happen to me, so trust me. I just don't want the police involved any earlier, that's all.

"I love you, but I've gotta go now. Thanks heaps. And if I don't see you before you get my message, don't worry, because I have everything under control." Sam tried not to appear too confident and gave Sue a quick hug before she left.

THE MERGER HEARING

"In a nutshell, mergers and acquisitions are important for the efficient functioning of the economy. They allow businesses to achieve efficiencies and diversify risk across a range of activities. However, the *Competition and Consumer Act* prohibits mergers that would have the effect, or be likely to have the effect, of substantially lessening competition in a market.

"Therefore, I need you three to drive home the argument that the benefits of this merger far outweigh the risk and the economy is the winner here. The alternative is potentially two failed businesses because these two businesses are not sustainable on their own."

Sam looked around the table. The three lawyers looked too afraid to say a word and simply nodded their heads in agreement.

She looked at them—Lyn Blackwood, Craig Evans, and Chris Tanners. Barry had picked the best, he'd said. They all looked a bit young to her, although she knew that all three were older than she was. Without her experience, of course.

Lyn was a startling woman to look at, with her red curls

constantly trying to escape the tight ponytail she kept them in, but her face was shrewd. She would get somewhere, Sam was sure.

Craig Evans looked a little too round-faced and innocent for her—almost like a cherub—but she had read enough on him to know that his looks were deceiving.

Chris Tanners was the most standard of the bunch—standard-looking and relatively standard-performing—but his attention to detail could be an asset and was why she assumed Barry had suggested him.

Not yet satisfied with their direction, Sam schooled them for almost another hour until she was convinced they were in sync with all her demands. Then she called for lunch to be delivered.

She watched as they perused the spread that had been laid out for them. On offer was Turkish and pita bread filled with an assortment of chicken and bacon salad, Mediterranean tuna, spicy chicken and prawns and a combination of other seafood with various sauces and condiments. A platter of fresh seasonal fruits rounded out the luncheon perfectly.

After demolishing a good portion of the food, the young lawyers began to unwind but once the champagne started flowing, they loosened up. That's when Sam really got to know them and reassured her that she had hired the right individuals for the task.

"Okay, team, listen up. Regarding the merger, you need to put this to bed tomorrow at the hearing. Make sure you avoid the approval being delayed for any reason. Remember, the economy is the winner here and there are no alternatives. The government bureaucrats will come up with some surprises so don't let them distract you from our game plan. I need you to do what we talked about. Do it in a polite and forthright manner and don't focus on their negative or worst-case scenarios and you will be fine.

"Try not to look over at me and make sure you all work together. Any questions before we finish up here?" Sam asked.

"No, we're all good," they answered.

"Good. Also, there's a cash bonus, on top of your fees, for each of you if you're successful tomorrow. I'll let you go and rest up for tomorrow. I will speak with you after the hearing."

———

The next morning, she arrived early at the government building in which the hearing was to take place and was thrilled to see her team were already there.

The public viewing area of the large contemporary venue was already half-full of reporters, interested stockholders and curious members of the public. A late news story on one of the main television networks had created interest in the hearing and seats were filling fast.

Fifteen minutes before the hearing was due to start, as Sam entered the room she felt a sharp pain in her right side near her waist. She turned to look behind her but there was no one nearby, so she placed her hand on her side as she took a seat in the back row. Her jacket felt wet and she looked down at her hand. It was covered in blood.

Immediately, she got up and made her way to the bathrooms to investigate. Once in the privacy of a toilet cubical, she removed her jacket and blouse to find a puncture wound on the right-hand side of her waist. It looked as if someone had tried to stab her but had botched the job.

The wound was not deep, and no serious damage had been done. Fortunately, she was wearing a dark navy suit which hid the bloodstains, but her ivory silk blouse was probably unsalvageable. However, a ruined blouse was the least of her problems. *Garza's men are here!*

After mentally retracing her steps, she decided it must have happened when she'd pushed her way out of the crowded elevator just before she'd entered the hearing room. She had no option but to leave immediately, especially with so many reporters present as she couldn't afford the media taking an interest in her.

Covering the wound with tissues and her handkerchief, she took off her stockings and wound them around her torso to hold her ad hoc dressing in place. Once she had washed the blood off her hands and straightened herself up, she looked in the mirror and took a deep breath to settle the rage growing inside.

Targeting her in such a public place showed Garza was getting desperate. Her attacker had not intended to kill her, or she would have been dead. Instead, they had planned to disable her and take her to Garza. Once she was in his clutches, it would only be a matter of time before they had the book glasses.

Upon exiting the bathroom, she strode along the hallway and took the stairs down, intentionally not looking back, despite knowing she was being followed. Her footsteps echoed around the empty stairwell and, once on ground level, she hid behind a large metal electrical cabinet, adjacent to the exit.

Her pursuers' footsteps grew louder and as she waited, it was apparent that there were at least three people giving chase. She put the book glasses back on, slipped off her stilettos and waited patiently.

When her first two pursuers arrived on the ground level, she stepped out in front of them and pointed to her glasses. "Are you looking for these? Come and get them, boys!"

"You're not tricking us again, bitch," Silverback said from

the stairs, and then to his thugs, "Get me those fucking glasses now!"

Before they could react, Sam struck out, one of her stiletto shoes in each hand. She ducked and weaved through the men's strikes until she made it through the defences of first one, then the other, stabbing them both in the throat. Leaving them incapacitated and bleeding on the floor, she turned her attention to Silverback, quickly dropping him with a sidekick to his neck.

"I'm not going to ask again, is Garza in Sydney or Italia?" Sam asked as she stood over him and watched him gasping for air.

"Sy-de-ney," he said, barely getting the word out.

"Where?" Sam asked, pressing the heel of her shoe into his throat.

"Thirty-second... Shangri-La!" he replied, breathing almost normally.

"Room number?"

"32... o... 8."

Before he had time to blink, Sam swung her arm back and drove her stiletto heel into his neck, killing him instantly. Then she wiped the blood off both of her heels onto his shirt and attached her shoes to her wrists via the slingback ankle straps.

But she couldn't leave the bodies in plain sight. They could be discovered at any time. She needed to be well clear of the building before that happened.

There was space under the stairs where the light didn't quite reach. She dragged each of her attackers around there. By the time she was finished, she was huffing and puffing and shook her head in dismay at the smeared blood trail that led to the shadowy recess. She may as well have erected a billboard saying, "Dead bodies this way".

She followed the hallway behind the stairs and found a door, but it was locked. The second one she came to was also locked, but when she tried the handle on the third, it opened. A mop was too much to hope for, but there were a couple of buckets and a sink.

She filled the buckets with water and used it to wash away the blood smears until there were only pink puddles of water left on the polished concrete floor. A final bucket of water rinsed away the pink, leaving the floor shiny and wet.

After stowing the buckets with the bodies, Sam put her shoes back on and exited the building via the doors at the bottom of the stairs.

Finding herself in a narrow laneway, she followed it along the building and back onto the busy street. Once she had put a couple of blocks between herself and the government building, she withdrew some cash from an ATM and, further down the block, stepped into a shop advertising fashion footwear. She quickly selected a pair of elegant navy suede pumps with stiletto heels and asked the retail assistant to retrieve a pair in her size. She paid in cash and left the shop and continued walking down the street.

At the entrance to the next alley, she stopped and took out her mobile phone and pretended to take a call. Upon confirming the alley was deserted, she headed down past a large dumpster. She opened the shoebox and placed the navy pumps on the ground, then removed her Jimmy Choo stilettos and slipped on the new shoes.

After wiping her Jimmy Choos down and shoving them into the shoebox, she flung it into the dumpster and walked away. Yes, they were gorgeous designer shoes that cost twelve hundred dollars, but they were also murder weapons and she could not afford to be caught wearing them.

She caught a bus to the upmarket Shangri-La Hotel. She was determined to put an end to Garza permanently, for Mr Harman, for Dr Dunn, and especially for Billy. The thought of

Billy and the dream of a life that because of Garza's greed would never be was a momentary distraction that she quickly thrust to the back of her mind.

Calmly and confidently, she made her way through the foyer to the lifts, eager to get this over and done without any further delay.

Upon exiting the elevator on the thirty-second floor, she noticed an unattended housekeeping trolley further down the hallway. A quick inspection revealed a spare apron and she put it on over her clothes and proceeded to push the trolley slowly up and down the hallway.

She didn't need to wait long. The door to his room opened and Garza appeared to attend to the hotel staff member delivering room service, loudly insisting he would not be letting anyone into his room. Keeping her head down to conceal her face, she pushed the trolley closer.

She felt a sharp pain in her shoulder, and she was grabbed from behind. She struggled against the strong arms that drew her back and pinned her against a large-muscled chest. Then everything went black.

KEEP THEM ON

Through the slowly dissipating fog in her mind, she could hear male voices yelling at each other in Italian and kept her eyes closed as she tried to figure out where she was.

She was no longer wearing the book glasses!

Then she remembered entering the Shangri-La Hotel looking for Garza. Apparently, she'd found him or, more accurately, he'd found her. She was sitting upright in what felt like a single leather lounge chair and was pleasantly surprised to discover no restraints on her arms or legs.

"Boss, it's been over five hours. She must be conscious by now!" one of the men said in Italian. "Maybe I should throw her under the shower to wake her up."

"How much ketamine did you inject into her, you son of a bitch?" another man asked, also in Italian.

"Shut the fuck up, you sons of bitches, can't you see I'm reading? I'm on the computer and the phone. These fucking glasses are working my ass off here, and I don't want to lose my focus because of you two fuckers. So help me God, I will kill you both if you don't shut the fuck up," Garza yelled back in Italian.

"Look, now you made the boss mad, you son of a bitch," one of the men said, lowering his voice as he walked away.

"Fuck you, you're the son of a bitch," the other whispered and followed him into the next room.

Sam wondered if Garza was feeling the side effects of wearing the glasses. If he'd been wearing them for the past five hours straight, then he probably was.

She opened her eyes slightly to get an idea of the layout of the room. She was in a lounge chair with a three-seater couch on her right and a side table to her left. On it were a few glasses and an empty champagne bottle. Garza was seated at a desk on the other side, engrossed in a computer screen.

And the thugs had walked out of the room and left the two of them by themselves while she was unrestrained. Garza needed to find better help.

Not one to waste an opportunity, Sam leapt out of her chair and pounced on him, hitting him on the back of the head with the champagne bottle. He slumped to the floor, out cold, still wearing the glasses. She then turned to the two thugs who came racing in and powered towards her like a pair of freight trains. She stepped to the side as the two fools dived for her, their momentum throwing them past her. She snatched up the side table and threw it at one and he crashed to the floor in a heap.

But the other had turned on her before she had the chance to do anything to him. She dodged behind some furniture, picking up Garza's chair and using it to keep him at bay while she looked for another weapon.

They both saw the gun at the same time, where it lay beside Garza. But Sam was closer, so she snatched it up and shot him in the chest. He sank to the floor, blood leaking from his torso.

Sam jumped over his body and checked the guard she had hit with the table. She wasn't sure he was dead, so she found some cord and tied him up.

She picked up Garza's chair and balanced it on his chest. With it bearing down on his neck and both arms, effectively locking him down hard, he quickly regained consciousness. Dazed, he looked up as a smiling Sam sat on the chair, side-saddle, looking down at him, while carelessly waving the Glock at him.

"*Buon giorno,* Signor Garza!" Sam said.

"*Parli Italiano!*" he said in shock.

"Sure do, shithead. So, you like my glasses?"

"They *mio bitcha!*" he replied in broken English.

"Well, if you want them, you keep them on!" Sam said and stuffed a large white dinner napkin into his mouth.

He thrashed about, trying to slip out from under the chair, so Sam threatened to put a bullet into each of his biceps if he didn't stop moving. Then, she sat there watching for the onset of the book glasses side effects.

Although she'd worn them once for as long as eight hours, which she believed had nearly killed her, she had found that five hours was the general limit for her. Five hours had come and gone for Garza, and this would be her opportunity to discover the full consequences of wearing them past the limits. And who better to use as a guinea pig?

An hour passed and the chair under her began to rock, slowly at first, but by the third hour, Garza was thrashing around uncontrollably. His eyes were closed, and he no longer took any notice of her threats to shoot him.

Even after realising blood was dripping from his eyes and down his cheeks, Sam still sat there, holding him down, waiting to see what would happen. Forty-five minutes later the chair, with Sam on it, was catapulted into the air and tossed halfway across the room. After landing on the lounge, feet first, Sam turned and saw Garza's body suspended two inches off the floor. Then blood started gushing out of his eyes, propelling the book glasses into the air. They landed next to her, covered in blood.

Sam didn't bother checking his body; it was clear he was dead. Shocked but not entirely surprised, she picked up the book glasses and took them into the bathroom.

After thoroughly cleaning the glasses and herself, she returned to the lounge but avoided looking at the carnage.

Taking another napkin from the table, she carefully cleaned her fingerprints off the Glock and placed it back in its dead owner's hand. Likewise, she wiped down what was left of the champagne bottle and the arms and backs of the chairs to remove any evidence linking her to the massacre.

She put on a black wig she found in the bathroom. With her head down to avoid hotel cameras, she strolled casually down the hall and slipped into the elevator. Exiting at ground level into a busy foyer, she made her way out of the building as quickly as possible without drawing attention to herself.

She slipped into a café next to the hotel and, after ordering her usual lemon tea and a glass of cold water, called Gower and Roth, and asked them to meet her there urgently. By the time she'd finished her beverages, the two detectives were there, waiting to hear the worst.

"Garza and four of his thugs are all dead. I don't know what happened. They grabbed me and injected me with something to knock me out and kidnapped me. When I came to hours later, I was lying on a lounge in a hotel room and then I discovered them... they were all dead."

She took a shaky breath and appeared to stare off into the distance. "There was so much blood... I was so scared. I quickly ran into the bathroom to hide. I waited for a while and, after not hearing a sound, I put on this wig I found in the bathroom and I got out of there. I came here and called you straight away." She put on a show of being rattled for the detectives' sake.

Gower said to Roth, "You stay with her while I take the uniforms up with me and check out the room." He turned to Sam. "What room number?"

"Room 3208."

DANGER IS OVER

Hours later, in an interrogation room on the ninth floor of the police headquarters, tired of all the questions from Gower and Roth, Sam just wanted to go home. "How many times do I need to repeat myself? There's nothing more I can tell you!" She was fed up with the questioning and she was not going to tolerate it any longer.

"Sorry, Dr Page, but what happened in that hotel room is hard to explain and anything you can tell us would go a long way to help us make some sense of the carnage," Roth said. "We are going to have a hard time explaining this."

"I don't know what happened because I was unconscious. I don't know any more than you do. I heard one of the men say they injected me with ketamine so I assume that will be confirmed when you get the results of the blood tests you asked for.

"Gentlemen, I've told you everything I know and now I'm leaving. However it happened, Garza is dead and if whoever killed Garza wanted me dead, they would have killed me. They had the perfect opportunity. So, the danger to me is over and

I'm finally going back to live my life without having to look over my shoulder anymore. Thank you for all your help and goodbye!"

Sam got up to leave but was stopped by Gower blocking the door. "Get out of my way, Detective."

"Before you go, Sam," Gower said, "with Garza dead, we hope that the threat to you is also gone but we cannot guarantee that is the case."

"What are you saying?"

"We suggest you continue to be vigilant regarding your safety and we would still like you to keep in touch with Detective Gower and myself." When Sam tried to interrupt, Roth held up his hand. "And Dr Page, if you refuse to consider your safety then perhaps you need to consider the safety of your unborn child."

Detective Gower and Roth seemed to fade away and it was almost as if she was back in her tiny studio apartment at the university.

"Billy, I have something important to tell you. Come here!" Sam called.

He was putting the kettle on to make a cup of tea. His eyes lit up. "Wait, don't tell me... you're pregnant?"

Sam was surprised by his answer. "No, you silly billy. I bought the Millennium apartment."

"Wow, that's awesome, but I thought you were moving in with me after your uni commitment finishes in six weeks?" He sounded a little disappointed.

"No, you know I want us to live in the city. I wanted to buy the penthouse, remember, but someone else gave them a better offer. Anyway, the apartment I just bought will do until the penthouse becomes available again. And when it does, it will not slip through my fingers a second time, that's for sure!"

"What about my place?"

"Now that it's paid off, how about we keep it for our weekend place. What do you think?"

"Sounds great. I'm happy if you're happy!" Billy said with his special smile.

"Thanks, honey! Anyway, what if I were pregnant?"

"Are you?" Billy's smile grew wider.

"No, of course not. But how would you feel if I were?"

"I would be the happiest guy in the world."

She smiled. "You know, I have loved you in all the wrong ways. Thank you, my darling, I will make it up to you soon."

His love warmed her heart. She was the luckiest woman in the world to have him.

He stepped forward to take her into his arms.

———

"Dr Page, are you alright? Dr Page? Hello!" Roth said, holding the door open for her.

Sam blinked a couple of times, not ready to leave her memories of Billy behind. Her eyes filled with tears at the reminder that he would never see their baby. "Yeah... what did you say?"

"We are waiting to take you home. Are you okay, doc?"

She wiped away the tears. "Sorry about that. Don't know what got into me."

"That's okay. This way back to the car and we'll get you home."

BACK TO BUSINESS

The silence in the car was deafening as the two detectives drove Sam back to her apartment. When they arrived outside, she hastily bid them goodbye, nodded to the security guard standing by her private elevator and headed upstairs.

After climbing out of a still-warm bath with the scent of bergamot clinging to her skin, Sam pulled on a pair of yoga pants and one of Billy's favourite T-shirts and ordered dinner from her favourite restaurant. It was a three-hat restaurant that, as a rule, didn't make deliveries, but Sam had come to an agreement with them, for a price, and the food was worth every cent.

Having thanked the delivery man, she sat down to her duck and cauliflower in red wine jus with salted grapes and a side of broccolini. She reached for a bottle of Grange Shiraz, a perfect match for the duck, when she remembered the baby and opted instead for a bottle of sparkling grape juice. Although definitely not a Grange, it was a refreshing drink and would not put her baby at risk.

She was glad to be home and eager to get back to business

first thing in the morning. She yawned as she finished her drink, so she headed off to bed. Exhausted, physically, and emotionally, as soon as her head hit the pillow, she slipped into a deep sleep.

———

The next morning, she had a 10 a.m. meeting scheduled with her team of lawyers to follow up on the merger approval and to congratulate them on a job well done. They had texted her the previous afternoon to inform her that the merger approval had been granted.

Before they arrived, she called Betty for an update and to inform her that she'd decided to fly over to Perth in the company jet later in the day to get the ball rolling on the merger.

"Welcome, please come in. I have morning tea ready in the boardroom and we can talk there," Sam said to the lawyers with a smile as they entered. "Please serve yourself. There are hot and cold beverages, warm croissants and an assortment of freshly baked muffins."

Once they had helped themselves to food and drink and each had taken a seat at the table, Sam said, "Who's going to update me on the proceedings of yesterday's hearing?"

Lyn Blackwood took the lead. "Ma'am, it was like clock-work. Everything went exactly as you said it would. We used your thirty-five-point plan as instructed without any resistance. We asked the panel to provide us with a set of guidelines to cross-reference with our understanding of them, which worked. We went through the points step by step and once the panel saw that our plan matched their guidelines, we had it in the bag."

"What about any other interests opposing the merger?" Sam asked, looking at the men for a response.

"There was no opposition whatsoever," said Craig.

"By 3 p.m. it was all done!" Lyn added.

"Outstanding!" She shook hands with each of them.

"Where were you? I thought you said you would be there all day," Lyn asked.

"I was... tied up, let's say... a bloody hectic situation!" She rolled her eyes. "Anyway, well done, team. Great work. Please eat up and enjoy."

"Sorry you missed it," said Lyn.

"Never mind. On another subject, I would like you three to join the Page Global team. If you are agreeable and are happy to work exclusively for me, I would be proud to have you all on board. With the merger approved, we have a lot of work to do to complete that project as well as other business in the works. Page Global needs to establish a good working relationship with a bank and we need to investigate our international law obligations."

Sam handed a folder of documents to each of the three. "Here are copies of your contracts for you to review if you are interested. You have a week to think about it and get back to me."

Again, Lyn took the lead after they all looked at the amount of the retainer just for agreeing to the contract. "I don't need any more time to think about it, Dr Page, I would all love to work for you. And I'd be happy to sign my contract now!"

"So would I," agreed Craig and Chris almost simultaneously.

"That's what I want to hear, great! Are you ready to start work tomorrow?"

They all nodded.

"Fantastic! I'm flying to Perth today and will contact you

from there. Once you have signed your contracts, I will immediately deposit your retainer into each of your accounts before I go. Again, well done and I'm looking forward to working with you." She shook each of their hands again.

After some more small talk, Lyn, Craig, and Chris walked out and into the elevator, leaving Sam extremely satisfied both with their accomplishment of achieving government approval for the merger and securing their services. She could now make her way to Perth to get the merger moving, knowing they would be available to back her up throughout the process.

No sooner had she transferred their retainers into their accounts she got changed, packed a bag, and grabbed an Uber to the airport. Her jet was already out on the private section of the busy airport tarmac with its engines running.

"How was the flight, Sam?" Betty asked, placing a huge pile of folders into her arms as the office staff relieved her of her handbag and travel luggage.

"Good thanks, Betty. What's all this? Can't you wait until I settle in first?" Sam asked.

"No time for that, sorry. I'm just following your instructions, remember," Betty replied, walking back to her desk.

Sam put on the book glasses to take in everything in the folders Betty had handed her. She was pleasantly surprised to discover Malcolm's intention, once the merger had been approved, was to increase coal production without incurring huge additional labour costs, which the company could ill-afford. The plan was well thought out and had merit.

She was also thrilled to discover that supply wasn't an issue and planned to meet with the industry's labour union to work out a deal to extend workers' shifts in the short-term as a way of keeping jobs. In return, a guarantee would be put in place to assure workers that once volume was up and yield targets achieved, shifts would go back to how they were, plus a four percent wage increase for each employee.

She needed to get the union representatives to understand that, without this deal, in less than twelve months the company would be bankrupt and all its employees out of work. All her capital was going into the merger, so this deal was simply about keeping Page Global employees in jobs for the long-term.

Sam quickly drafted a letter and forwarded it to her team in Sydney, who established contact with union officials and arranged a meeting at the Perth office in two days' time.

Betty insisted Sam stay at her place for the night and they stopped for dinner at a Yum Cha restaurant near her home. Over a smorgasbord of delicious dim sum along with Chinese tea, they talked mostly about Malcolm.

"After my husband died from lung cancer almost ten years ago, Malcolm and his wife, Alice, were very supportive and that's when I got close to Alice," said Betty. "Around about the same time, she started working in the office with Malcolm, but the constant closeness ended up being too much and it was the beginning of the end of their marriage.

"They split up twice. The first time was almost five years ago and the second and final time was last year. It was after their first breakup that our affair began, but it didn't last long."

Sam hid her surprise at Betty's openness. "And Malcolm and Alice got back together after you split up? That must have been hard for you."

"Yes, by the time they got back together, we had ended our affair and didn't bring it up again. When they separated for good last year, Malcolm was initially so distraught that I kept away from him, waiting for him to make the first move... but I waited too long," Betty whispered, sipping on her green jasmine tea.

"Sorry, Betty. You loved him, didn't you?" Sam said.

"I guess I did," she admitted.

It struck Sam as sad that Betty hadn't made Malcolm aware of how she'd felt about him or tried to reignite their relationship.

Back at Betty's house, Sam thanked her for sharing her battle with her. Their surprisingly intimate conversation had distracted her from the concerns of her upcoming meeting with the union officials.

Also, not once that evening had Sam thought about the lowlife Antonios Garza, who nearly got away with not only the book glasses but also the murder of Mr Harman, Dr Dunn, and her beloved Billy. Now that Garza was forever out of her life, for the first time since taking possession of the glasses, it felt strange for her to not be looking over her shoulder. A sense of peacefulness washed over her and the thought that no one else would try to take them from her brought a smile to her face.

———

The next morning Sam and Betty picked up breakfast on the way into the office. Then, working with her team in Sydney, they finalised the proposal, and they set up the boardroom for video conferencing to allow her team to participate in the meeting as a show of strength to intimidate the union officials.

The meeting came and went without any hitches, with the union officials agreeing to all her requests. As soon as they left, and before shutting down the video link, Sam decreed that celebrations were in order and asked for the champagne that had been delivered to the Perth office and her team in Sydney especially for the occasion, be opened immediately.

As she enjoyed a glass of bubbly with her team on both coasts, she felt she had it all. Looking around with a smile from ear to ear, she envisaged a wealthy future beyond her dreams and was determined that nothing and no one would stop her from achieving it.

YOU KILLED MY FATHER

Sam stayed another two days with Betty as they both arranged the purchase of an apartment in Perth for Sam before flying back to Sydney. En route from the airport via an Uber, she checked in with Lyn, Craig, and Chris to inform them of her return.

Back in her Sydney apartment, Sam walked into her boardroom to drop off the meeting's documents. She screamed at the scene before her. Sister Sue was tied to one of the chairs, bruised and battered and crying profusely.

"About time, mademoiselle, we've been waiting for you!" a well-groomed man bellowed in a mixed Australian and French accent. He wore black trousers and his white shirt sleeves were rolled up to reveal tanned forearms. With one hand he grabbed Sister Sue by her hair and with the other, he held a knife to her throat.

"Who are you and what have you done to Sister Sue? Who sent you?" Sam yelled as her briefcase and the documents she held dropped to the floor.

"I will be asking the questions, *mon cheri*," he said, gliding the blunt edge of the blade across the skin of Sue's throat, back and forth, almost like a dare.

"Sister Sue, what are you doing here?" Sam asked.

"I was waiting for your text, and I got worried, so I came here to see if you were okay, and he opened the—" A vicious blow to the side of Sue's face abruptly cut her off.

"Leave her alone, you fucker! I'm sorry, Sue, I forgot all about you. Everything is fine now," Sam said, horrified that she'd put her in harm's way.

Without looking at Sam, the man calmly turned the blade over and rested it on Sue's neck, at the same time using his other hand to mime what looked like a spray of blood coming from Sue's throat.

"Okay, okay, please don't hurt her. I will tell you anything you want," Sam said.

The man turned toward her. "I'm not going to hurt her. I'm going to kill her!"

"Why would you want to kill a nun?" Sam asked, more confused than ever.

"You killed my father so I will kill your mother," the deranged man stated, his eyes filled with hatred.

"You must be mistaken! Who's your father? And Sister Sue is a nun. She's not my mother."

"Antonios Garza was my father and you murdered him. As for your mother, she and I have been here for some time now waiting for your return, and we have got to know each other quite well. The Bible says an eye for an eye and a tooth for a tooth."

"But, in the New Testament, Matthew 5:38–42 says, 'But I say unto you, that ye resist not evil: but whosoever shall smite thee on thy right cheek, turn to him the other also.'"

"Impressive, but it won't save your mother," he said, taking the knife away from Sue's throat and pointing it at Sam.

"Why would you think I killed your father?" Sam asked, trying to buy more time.

"I know you killed him with those glasses you have on, and soon you will suffer and endure my pain before I kill you too. You see, I know everything, so there's no escape for you. Now you will watch your mother die." He calmly turned back and stood next to Sue.

"What is he talking about, Sue?" Sam asked.

Sue looked up at Sam, and with tears streaming from her eyes said in a voice filled with pain and weariness, "I'm sorry, my girl, but I've been afraid to tell you all these years. Do you forgive me? You have always been the love of my life."

"What are talking about? You can't be my mother! My mother died when I was a baby." She turned to Garza Junior and pleaded, "Look, she doesn't know what she's saying. Wait... wait, here, take the glasses. Please take them and leave us alone." In total despair, Sam stared into Sue's eyes.

"Yeah, I will take the glasses, once you are both dead. I will take them off your cold corpse with pleasure," he said nonchalantly.

"*Monsieur, je n'ai pas tué votre père, mais si vous la tuez, je ne vous dirai jamais qui l'a fait!*" Sam said[1].

"Your French is very good. Okay, now you have my attention. Tell me who killed my father. I will know if you're lying."

"Your father's men knocked me out and kidnapped me, and when I woke up hours later on the lounge in his apartment at the Shangri-La, I saw what looked like flames shooting out of his eyes. He was wearing the book glasses. Now, the glasses have certain restrictions, and they will not allow you to keep them on for any lengthy period. If you disregard these warning signs, you will not live to regret it. It was the book glasses that killed your father," Sam said. "Can I ask your name, please?"

"My name is Anthony Garza," he replied. "Did you know my father was a priest?"

Sam shook her head but didn't say a word, silently prompting him to continue talking. She moved around the room, trying to creep closer.

"He left the priesthood before I was born and from then on, lived his life differently from how he was brought up. He became a bent and twisted man as a result of searching for those glasses.

"Growing up, I thought they were a myth. He always kept me at a distance, something I never understood until I was a man and realised he was responsible for doing the most appalling and diabolical things to people who crossed him.

"During those rare visits I received from him as a child, he would tell me stories of the holy glasses and the powers they have. I always loved when he would tell me about all the bad stuff that would happen to anyone who wore them beyond their limits. He was aware that there were limits regarding the time one could wear the glasses, so I suspect there is something you are not telling me. But the details don't matter now. I hold you personally responsible for his death."

"Okay, kill me, but why hurt an innocent nun who thinks she is my mother?"

"YOU KILLED MY FATHER. I'M KILLING YOUR MOTHER!" he screamed in rage.

As he'd talked, Sam had inched closer and when he finished screaming at her, she pounced. In contrast to his father, Garza Junior had a slim build and stood no taller than five foot four, so after kicking the knife out of his hands and knocking him to the floor, she effortlessly held him down with her foot against his throat.

But he grabbed her ankle and, with a strength that belied his small frame, forced Sam backwards until she found herself flat on her back on the floor. He leapt on top of her and wrapped his hands around her throat.

As she gasped for breath, she realised he intended to choke her to death. His aggressiveness and strength took her by surprise. As the room around her faded and she succumbed to unconsciousness, her last thoughts turned to Sue. *Sorry I couldn't protect you...*

"Samantha! Wake up. I'm not going to let you get out of it that easily," said Garza. "Before you die, you will watch your mother die."

Sam jerked and cried out at the intense burning pain in her shoulder. She opened her eyes to see Garza withdraw the bloody blade of his knife from her shoulder. Blood soaked into her sleeve and dripped onto the floor. Her neck and throat ached but they were secondary compared with the pain radiating from her shoulder.

"Will that keep you awake long enough to watch your mother take her last breaths?" He toyed with her by gently running the tip of his knife from her shoulder, across her collar bone, to her throat.

"No, don't hurt her anymore," begged Sue.

When Garza glanced over at Sue, taking advantage of his momentary distraction, Sam flicked the knife out of his hand and then head-butted him and tried to push him off her, without any success. Pain exploded in her forehead and she felt dazed. Perhaps headbutting wasn't such a great idea after all? She'd never trained for it.

Garza shook his head and blinked a couple of times before focusing his rage squarely on Sam. "You little bitch," he yelled. "You are going to regret that." Again, he encircled her neck with his hands and this time he shook her like a rag doll as he tightened his grip.

Thrashing about, Sam desperately tried to suck air into her lungs but his vice-like grip cut off her airway. Panic rose in her as she tried to prise his fingers off her throat. Darkness began to encroach. She tried to fight it, but the darkness won.

———

"Sam, Sam, can you hear me?" Sue cried, tears streaming freely down her face.

Sam opened her eyes and looked up at her. "What... what happened?" she asked hoarsely.

"It's okay. You're safe now."

When she tried to sit up, the intense pain shooting through her shoulder made her gasp and she slumped back onto the floor.

Sue pressed down on her shoulder with a blood-stained tea towel. "Just lie back down and you'll be okay. The ambulance is on its way, so you just stay there and don't worry about a thing."

"Where's...?" Sam's eyes darted around the room.

Sue took her hand. "Relax, he's gone. Two detectives came in and arrested that madman before he choked you to death."

She looked around to see police swarming throughout her apartment.

"Look what he's done to your face! I'm so sorry, Sue." Sam reached up to gently touch the small part of the nun's face that wasn't covered in bruises.

"I'm fine now that I know you are okay. I love you, Sam!" She said, crying and kissing both of Sam's hands.

"I love you too, Mum!" said Sam, teary-eyed.

"So, you know?" Sue asked, a hopeful light in her eyes.

"I've known all along in my heart from the first day I met

you, at eighteen. But it was the book glasses that helped me to research and confirm my suspicions. By then, it didn't matter as long as you were in my life, so I continued with the game," Sam said with a smile.

"I'm sorry, my love. I was afraid you would be angry at me for leaving you at such a young age, that you would push me away after just coming back into my life again. I couldn't bear to lose you. And then, as time passed, the longer I left telling you, the harder it was to bring it up."

"It's okay. I know all about the crash and especially about how unwell both you and Aunty Joyce were. You don't need to explain it to me."

"Thank you, my love."

Detective Roth knelt on the other side of Sam. "Dr Page, it's good to see you are okay. The ambulance is only minutes away and it would be best if you stay where you are until the ambos check you out. As you can see, Sister Sue needs to be taken care of as well, so be patient. They won't be long."

"How did you know Garza's son was at my apartment?" Sam asked.

"We didn't. You weren't answering your phone so we called Betty and she said you should be home by now, so we came straight here to go over your police statement from the other day. Once we gained access, we found that maniac choking you to death," Roth replied with a grin.

"Where is he?"

It was Gower who answered from behind Roth. "Don't worry about Garza's son. We've handed him over to the uniforms who have taken him away to charge him with attempted murder, amongst other things, so he won't be bothering you again."

Two ambulance officers appeared in the doorway and Gower waved them over. The detectives waited until Sam and

Sue were both in the ambulance and followed them to the hospital. As the two women held each other, a sense of happiness and fulfilment flowed over Sam and she knew that things were going to be different for her now she knew she had a family of her own.

FAMILY OF MY OWN

They had to stay in overnight as the hospital wanted to monitor the baby and Sue had a concussion. Once they were both given the all-clear, Sam took Sue back to her apartment.

Even though her apartment had been thoroughly cleaned to remove all evidence of the violence that had occurred, she held her breath when they walked in. But it was as if the blood, brutality, and death had just been a bad dream.

Sue was still overwhelmed by what had happened so Sam led her into one of the spare bedrooms and phoned in an order for lunch to be delivered.

"Lunch will be here soon," she said. But when Sam went into Sue's room, her heart was filled with joy and such a mix of emotions that she couldn't speak.

Sue seemed confused by her reaction. "Come here, my love. What's the matter?"

"I'm so happy that I finally have a family of my own."

"Well, if that's how you feel about ordering me lunch, I can't wait to see how you react when the baby gives you dirty nappies." Sue gave her a hug and a kiss.

Sam headed to the kitchen to put on the kettle, still smiling in wonder at thought of having a family—a mother and soon a child of her own.

As she walked through the lounge room, she reached down to straighten one of the lounge cushions. When she moved it, she noticed a pair of glasses wedged down into the back of the lounge. What were her book glasses doing there? But they didn't quite look like her glasses as the frames were a darker grey.

With her heart racing, Sam ran to her handbag and pulled out her book glasses. Comparing the two sets, she was shocked at how alike they were. If not for the slightly different shades of grey in their frames, it would be nearly impossible to pick hers from the set.

The doorbell rang, and she opened the door still holding both sets of glasses.

"Lunch delivery for Page," a young man said, holding out two plastic bags.

"Yes, thank you." She took the bags from him and closed the door.

She dropped the plastic bags on the kitchen bench and ran into her bedroom to hide the two sets of glasses, horrified that she had opened the door to let a stranger in while holding them.

"Who was at the door, Sam?" Sue called out from the bedroom.

"The delivery man. Our lunch is here. Are you hungry?" Sam replied as she walked back into the kitchen.

"I'm starving. What do we have here?" Sue walked over to the plastic bags to investigate the irresistible aromas.

"No, you take a seat at the table and I will bring it all over to you, okay?"

"These are delicious. I've never tasted sandwiches like this before. The fillings are divine. Thank you, my love."

"You're welcome and if you like this, you are going to love what I've ordered to have afterwards with a cup of tea."

"Thank you. You bring me so much joy."

"This is what families do; they take care of each other," Sam replied.

Sam asked Sue to tell her more about her life and loved listening to her stories about how she'd met her father and how Sue's sister, Joyce, had been such a big part of her life, especially after the tragic accident that had claimed Nicole and both their husbands.

When the subject turned to Sam, she avoided talking about her experiences in foster care and kept the conversation mostly about the almost comical mishaps that had occurred while she had been volunteering at the refuge.

Later, while Sue took an afternoon nap, Sam retrieved the two sets of glasses from their hiding spot. Taking a deep breath, she put on the new set of glasses and opened a book from a pile on her bedside table. She could read the words just as clearly as if she had been wearing her glasses.

There were two sets of book glasses! But where had the second set come from? And how had they ended up in her loungeroom?

Still shaken from her discovery, she phoned and left messages for both Gower and Roth to request a few minutes with Anthony Garza. He must have dropped the glasses while waiting for her to return to her apartment. It was a long shot, but perhaps she could provoke the deranged criminal enough to prompt him to tell her where he'd got the second pair of glasses.

When Gower called back, Sam convinced him to give her five minutes with Garza later that same afternoon as he had been transported to police headquarters in the city for further questioning.

Sam stowed both sets of glasses in her handbag and went to

her mother's room to find Sue lying on the bed. "Are you awake, Mum?"

"Yes, my love," Sue said, sounding half-asleep.

"I need to go out and sort out some business matters, but I'll be back as soon as I can."

"I'm fine, my love. You take your time and do what you need to do."

"If you need anything, please call me. I won't be long." Sam gave her a quick kiss on her cheek and headed out.

A SECOND PAIR OF GLASSES

Two pairs of book glasses?

As she walked through the city, Sam contemplated what she had achieved with one set of glasses and imagined the possibilities of having two motivated people working together, both with the power of the book glasses.

But how had Garza Junior got his hands on them? She recollected Gower and Roth telling her of Garza's trail of destruction over the decades and was devastated to think that he or his son could have used the second pair of glasses to achieve his evil aims.

Sam needed to know about the second set of glasses and the only way she could get answers was to meet with Anthony Garza face to face. She needed to get him to admit that the second pair were his and tell her where he'd got them. But to do so she needed to be fearless as he would sense her fear of him and use it against her. Therefore, she consciously pushed aside any residual fear she was still holding onto regarding the man who had nearly killed her and her mother.

By the time she'd arrived at police headquarters in the heart of the city, she was ready for the challenge. She had even rehearsed the questions she had for him in her head. Gower and Roth were both there to meet her in the foyer and first escorted her to their office to brief her about keeping the meeting short and to avoid creating a scene.

"Allowing you to meet with Garza is irregular and we would prefer that you do not draw any unwanted attention to yourself or this meeting. And you mustn't give Garza any grounds to accuse us of violating his rights in any way or to mistake this meeting as abuse or harassment. Do you understand?" said Gower.

"Yes," said Sam. "Message received loud and clear."

"Please wait here while we escort Garza from the holding cells to an interview room."

Fifteen minutes later, Roth returned and led her to the interview room where Garza was sitting alone at a table carefully restrained for her safety. She assumed the two detectives would take their place behind the two-way mirror to watch and listen to the meeting without being seen. Therefore, she knew she must watch her words, not just for Garza's sake, but to avoid contradicting the story she had already told the detectives.

When Garza looked up and recognised her, his face darkened with loathing. "What the fuck are you doing here?"

"Look, I didn't kill your father. It was his hatred, evilness and greed that killed him," Sam said.

"I know you killed my father."

"I will do a deal with you. Tell me where you got these glasses, and I will tell you the truth about your father's death." She retrieved the second pair of book glasses from her handbag and showed them to him.

"The truth is you fucking killed him, you fucking bitch and, if I wasn't handcuffed, I would kill you myself."

"Okay, if you don't want to hear about his death, fine. It will remain my secret and you will never know the truth."

"Wait, bitch. Tell me, what secret?"

"First, you tell me where you got these glasses, and I will tell you the truth about your father's death."

"What are you talking about? I didn't have the glasses. They are the glasses you had all along."

"Okay, if you want to be like that, I'm walking."

"No, wait. I'm telling you the truth. If I already had the glasses, why would my father and I have gone to so much trouble to track you down to get them?"

"You need to do better than that. I found these glasses in my apartment. Remember? The place where you almost choked me to death. You're full of shit. I'll give you one last chance, tell me about these glasses or I'm out of here and you will never know the truth about your father's death."

Garza looked bewildered. "Why would I lie? I didn't have the glasses when I went to your apartment. Now tell me about my father. Please!"

Without another word, Sam turned and walked out the door, frustrated and confused. She was beginning to believe that Garza was telling the truth.

As she closed the door, the next door in the hallway opened and Gower appeared. "Before you go can we see you in here, please?" He let her into the viewing room where they could see Garza throwing a mini tantrum and fighting against his restraints. But he wasn't going anywhere.

"What's up? I'm finished with him. He's of no use to me. He's going to take it to his grave," Sam said angry and frustrated as she pointed at him through the window.

"Garza's son doesn't know anything about the glasses because it was not him who left them in your apartment," Roth said.

"I found these glasses in my apartment. The same place he held my mother captive for over twenty-four hours and where he tried to kill me and her. Who else could have left them there? No one else was in my apartment."

"There was, actually," Roth said.

"What are you talking about?" asked Sam, her anger rising.

"Calm down. We were asked to look for a pair of glasses, but we've been so busy, we hadn't got around to doing that," Gower replied.

"Asked to look for them? By whom?"

"The glasses belong to your mother, Sister Sue. It was she who told us to look for them," Roth explained.

"What?" Sam couldn't believe her ears. Her entire world then went into a tailspin. She was transported back to the time she had first told her mother about the book glasses and recalled how easily Sue had believed her incredible story and how cautionary she had been. She had insisted that the glasses belonged to the Catholic church and needed to be returned. And Sue knew all about the side effects, the visions. It all made sense now.

Her emotions were like a whirlwind swirling inside her and she reached out to the wall with both hands to keep herself from falling. She hardly noticed Roth and Gower approach her from each side to help hold her up.

The knowledge that she had been spectacularly deceived was earth-shattering. Shaken to her core, she felt her mother's betrayal pierce her like a dagger to the heart. Clearly, Sue had kept much more from her than the fact that she was her mother. What other secrets had she kept?

"Excuse me, Sam. Hello, can you hear me?" Gower shouted, still holding her up on one side.

"Let's put her down on the chair. She's in shock!" Roth demanded.

"I'm calling the ambos. She's as white as a ghost!"

"No, give her a minute or two. Let's see how she goes. She's got the bloody holy glasses; she been lying to us all this time. If we'd known her mother was talking about them, we wouldn't have wasted all this time. Now there are two pairs of them, so let's wait until she snaps out of it. I want those glasses so go get her some water. I'll hold her here in the chair."

This was not what Sam had expected. And the woman who she knew as Sister Sue, who claimed to be her mother, might have other motives for her actions.

Regardless of what possibilities tomorrow might bring for Samantha Page, she needed the truth.

Dear reader,

We hope you enjoyed reading *The Book Glasses*. Please take a moment to leave a review, even if it's a short one. Your opinion is important to us.

Discover more books by Arthur Bozikas at
https://www.nextchapter.pub/authors/arthur-bozikas

Want to know when one of our books is free or discounted? Join the newsletter at
http://eepurl.com/bqqB3H

Best regards,

Arthur Bozikas and the Next Chapter Team